IN HARRY HARRISON'S STRANGE
WORLDS OF THE FUTURE,
YOU'LL MEET:

* The finest hunter in the world – and his
bizarre prey. . . .

* The astronauts who returned from the
Moon and ran smack into a time-warp. . . .

* The Ghoul Squad, who always seemed to be
first on the scene of disaster. . . .

* The radio that ran on gravity. . . .

* The man who cracked the riddle of
Stonehenge – and set the world an unsolvable
problem. . . .

NINETEEN MINDBENDING STORIES –
A FEAST OF SCIENCE FICTION!

Prime Number

HARRY HARRISON

SPHERE BOOKS LIMITED
30/32 Gray's Inn Road, London WC1X 8JL

First published in Great Britain by Sphere Books Ltd, 1975
Copyright © Harry Harrison 1970
Reprinted 1978, 1983 (twice)

TRADE
MARK

Set in Intertype Times

Printed in Great Britain by
Hazell Watson & Viney Limited,
Member of the BPCC Group,
Aylesbury, Bucks

CONTENTS

ACKNOWLEDGMENTS

"Mute Milton", copyright © 1966 by Ultimate Publishing Co., Inc.

"The Greatest Car in the World", copyright © 1966 by New Worlds SF.

"The Final Battle", copyright © 1970 by Harry Harrison.

"The Powers of Observation", copyright © 1968 by The Condé Nast Publications, Inc.

"Toy Shop", copyright © 1962 by The Condé Nast Publications, Inc.

"You Men of Violence", copyright © 1967 by Galaxy Publishing Corp.

"The Finest Hunter in the World", copyright © 1970 by Harry Harrison.

"Down to Earth", copyright © 1963 by Ziff-Davis Publishing Company.

"Not Me, Not Amos Cabot!", copyright © 1965 by Nova Publications Ltd.

"The Secret of Stonehenge", copyright © 1968 by Mercury Press, Inc.

"Incident in the IND", copyright © 1964 by Mercury Press, Inc.

"If", copyright © 1968 by Galaxy Publishing Corp. Originally titled *Praiseworthy Saur*.

"Contact Man", copyright © 1966 by Harry Harrison.

"The Pad", copyright © 1970 by Harry Harrison.

"A Civil Service Servant", copyright © 1967 by Galaxy Publishing Corp. Originally titled *The Fairly Civil Service*.

"A Criminal Act", copyright © 1966 by The Condé Nast Publications, Inc.

"Famous First Words", copyright © 1964 by Mercury Press, Inc.

"The Ghoul Squad", copyright © 1969 by The Condé Nast Publications, Inc.

"Commando Raid", copyright © 1970 by Harry Harrison.

MUTE MILTON

With ponderous smoothness the big Greyhound bus braked to a stop at the platform and the door swung open. "Springville," the driver called out; "last stop!" The passengers stirred in the aisle and climbed down the steps into the glare of the sun. Sam Morrison sat patiently, alone, on the wide rear seat, waiting until the last passengers were at the door before he put the cigar box under his arm, rose, and followed them. The glare of sunlight blinded him after the tinted-glass dimness of the bus, and the moist air held the breathless heat of Mississippi summer. Sam went carefully down the steps one-at-a-time, watching his feet, and wasn't aware of the man waiting there until something hard pushed at his stomach.

"What business yuh got in Springville, boy?"

Sam blinked through his steel-rimmed glasses at the big man in the gray uniform who stood before him, prodding him with a short, thick nightstick. He was fat as well as big, and the smooth melon of his stomach bulged out over his belt, worn low about his hips.

"Just passing through, sir," Sam Morrison said and took his hat off with his free hand, disclosing his cut short grizzled hair. He let his glance slide across the flushed red-dened face and the gold badge on the shirt before him, then lowered his eyes.

"An just where yuh goin to, boy? Don' keep no secrets from me . . ." the voice rasped again.

"Carteret, sir, my bus leaves in an hour."

The only answer was an uncommunicative grunt. The lead-weighted stick tapped on the cigar box under Sam's

7

arm. "What yuh got in there—a gun?"

"No, sir, I wouldn't carry a gun." Sam opened the cigar box and held it out: it contained a lump of metal, a number of small electronic components and a two-inch speaker, all neatly wired and soldered together. "It's a . . . a radio, sir."

"Turn it on."

Sam threw a switch and made one or two careful adjustments. The little speaker rattled and there was the squeak of tinny music barely audible above the rumble of bus motors. The red-faced man laughed.

"Now that's what Ah call a real nigger radio . . . piece uh trash." His voice hardened again. "See that you're on that bus, hear?"

"Yes, sir," Sam said to the receding. sweat-stained back of the shirt, then carefully closed the box. He started toward the colored waiting room but when he passed the window and looked in he saw that it was empty. And there were no dark faces visible anywhere on the street. Without changing pace Sam passed the waiting room and threaded his way between the buses in the cinder parking lot and out of the rear gate. He had lived all of his sixty-seven years in the State of Mississippi so he knew at once that there was trouble in the air—and the only thing to do about trouble was to stay away from it. The streets became narrower and dirtier and he trod their familiar sidewalks until he saw a field worker in patched overalls turn into a doorway ahead under the weathered "Bar" sign. Sam went in after him; he would wait here until a few minutes before the bus was due.

"Bottle of Jax, please." He spread his coins on the damp, scratched bar and picked up the cold bottle. There was no glass. The bartender said nothing. After ringing up the sale he retired to a chair at the far end of the bar with his head next to the murmuring radio and remained there, dark and impenetrable. The only light came from the street outside, and the high-backed booths in the rear looked cool and inviting. There were only a few other customers here, each of them sitting separately with a bottle of beer on the table before him. Sam threaded his way through the close-spaced tables and had already started to slide into the booth near the rear door when he noticed that someone was already there, seated on the other side of the table.

"I'm sorry, I didn't see you," he said and started to get up, but the man waved him back onto the bench and took an airline bag with "TWA" on it from the table and put it down beside him.

"Plenty of room for both," he said and raised his bottle of beer. "Here's looking at you." Sam took a sip from his own bottle, but the other man kept drinking until he had drained half of his before he lowered it with a relaxed sigh. "That's what I call foul beer," he said.

"You seem to be enjoying it," Sam told him, but his slight smile took the edge from his words.

"Just because it's cold and wet—but I'd trade a case of it for a bottle of Bud or a Ballantine."

"Then you're from the North, I imagine?" Sam had thought so from the way he talked, sharp and clipped. Now that his eyes were getting used to the dimness he could see that the other was a young man in his twenties with medium-dark skin, wearing a white shirt with rolled-up sleeves. His face was taut and the frown wrinkles on his forehead seemed etched there.

"You are damned right, I'm from the North and I'm going back . . ." he broke off suddenly and took another swig of beer. When he spoke again his voice was cautious. "Are you from these parts?"

"I was born not far from here, but right now I live in Carteret, just stopping off here between buses."

"Carteret—that's where the college is, isn't it?"

"That is correct. I teach there."

The younger man smiled for the first time. "That sort of puts us in the same boat, I go to NYU, majoring in economics." He put his hand out. "Charles Wright —everyone but my mother calls me Charlie."

"Very pleased to meet you," Sam said in his slow old-fashioned way. "I am Sam Morrison, and it is Sam on my birth certificate too."

"I'm interested in your college, I meant to stop in there but . . ." Charles broke off suddenly at the sound of a car's engine in the street outside and leaned forward so that he could see out the front door, remaining there until the car ground into gear and moved away. When Charles dropped back onto the seat Sam could see that there were fine beads of sweat in the lines of his forehead. He took a quick drink from his bottle.

"When you were at the bus station you didn't happen to see a big cop with a big gut, red face all the time?"

"Yes, I met him, he talked to me when I got off the bus."

"The bastard!"

"Don't get worked up, Charles; he is just a policeman doing his job."

"Just a . . . !" The young man spat a short, filthy word. "That's Brinkley, you must have heard of him, toughest man south of Bombingham. He's going to be elected sheriff next fall and he's already a Grand Knight of the Klan, a real pillar of the community."

"Talking like that's not going to do you any good," Sam said mildly.

"That's what Uncle Tom said—and as I remember he was still a slave when he died. Someone has got to speak up, you can't remain quiet forever."

"You talk like one of those Freedom Riders." Sam tried to look stern, but he had never been very good at it.

"Well I *am* one, if you want to know the truth of it, but the ride ends right here. I'm going home. I'm scared and I'm not afraid to admit it. You people live in a jungle down here; I never realized how bad it could be until I came down. I've been working on the voter's committee and Brinkley got word of it and swore he was going to kill me or put me in jail for life. And you know what?—I believe it. I'm leaving today, just waiting for the car to pick me up. I'm going back North where I belong."

"I understand you have your problems up there too . . ."

"Problems!" Charlie finished his beer and stood up. "I wouldn't even call them problems after what I've seen down here. It's no paradise in New York—but you stand a chance of living a bit longer. Where I grew up in South Jamaica we had it rough, but we had our own house in a good neighborhood and—you take another beer?"

"No, one is enough for me, thank you."

Charlie came back with a fresh beer and picked up where he had left off. "Maybe we're second-class citizens in the North—but at least we're citizens of some kind and can get some measure of happiness and fulfillment. Down here a man is a beast of burden and that's all he is ever going to be—if he has the wrong color skin."

"I wouldn't say that, things get better all the time. My father was a field hand, a son of a slave—and I'm a college teacher. That's progress of a sort."

"What sort?" Charlie pounded the table, yet kept his voice in an angry whisper. "So one hundreth of one percent of the Negroes get a little education and pass it on at some backwater college. Look, I'm not running you down; I know you do your best. But for every man like you there must be a thousand who are born and live and die in filthy poverty, year after year, without hope. Millions of people. Is that progress? And even yourself—are you sure you wouldn't be doing better if you were teaching in a decent university?"

"Not me," Sam laughed. "I'm just an ordinary teacher and I have enough trouble getting geometry and algebra across to my students without trying to explain topology or Boolean algebra or anything like that."

"What on eath is that Bool . . . thing? I never heard of it."

"It's, well, an uninterpreted logical calculus, a special discipline. I warned you, I'm not very good at explaining these things though I can work them out well enough on paper. That is my hobby, really, what some people call higher mathematics; and I know that if I were working at a big school I would have no time to devote to it."

"How do you know? Maybe they would have one of those big computers—wouldn't that help you?"

"Perhaps, of course, but I've worked out ways of getting around the need for one. It takes a little more time, that's all."

"And how much time do you have left?" Charlie asked quietly, then was instantly sorry he had said it when he saw the older man lower his head without answering. "I take that back, I've got a big mouth, I'm sorry. But I get so angry. How do you know what you might have done if you had had the training, the facilities . . ." He shut up, realizing that he was getting in deeper every second.

There was only the murmur of distant traffic in the hot,

dark silence, the faint sound of music from the radio behind the bar. The bartender stood, switched the radio off, and opened the trap behind the bar to bring up another case of beer. From nearby the sound of the music continued like a remembered echo. Charlie realized that it was coming from the cigar box on the table before them.

"Do you have a radio in that?" he asked, happy to change the subject.

"Yes—well really no, though there is an RF stage."

"If you think you're making sense—you're not. I told you, I'm majoring in economics."

Sam smiled and opened the box, pointing to the precisely wired circuits inside. "My nephew made this, he has a little 'I-fix-it' shop, but he learned a lot about electronics in the air force. I brought him the equations and we worked out the circuit together."

Charlie thought about a man with electronic training who was forced to run a handyman's shop, but he had the sense not to mention it. "Just what is it supposed to do?"

"It's not really supposed to do anything, I just built it to see if my equations would work out in practice. I suppose you don't know much about Einstein's unified field theory . . . ?" Charlie smiled ruefully and raised his hands in surrender. "It's difficult to talk about. Putting it the simplest way, there is supposed to be a relation between all phenomena, all forms of energy and matter. You are acquainted with the simpler interchanges, heat energy to mechanical energy as in an engine, electrical energy to light . . ."

"The light bulb!"

"Correct. To go further, the postulation has been made that time is related to light energy, as is gravity to light, which has been proved, and gravity to electrical energy. That is the field I have been exploring. I have made certain suppositions that there is an interchange of energy within a gravitic field, a measurable interchange, such as the lines of force that are revealed about a magnetic field by iron particles—ro, that's not a good simile—perhaps the ability of a wire to carry a current endlessly under the chilled condition of superconductivity—"

"Professor, you have lost me, I'm not ashamed to admit it. Could you maybe give me an example—like what is happening in this little radio here?"

Sam made a careful adjustment and the music gained the tiniest amount of volume. "It's not the radio part that is interesting, that stage really just demonstrates that I have detected the leakage—no, we should call it the differential—between the earth's gravitic field and that of the lump of lead there in the corner of the box."

"Where is the battery?"

Sam smiled proudly. "*That* is the point—there is no battery. The input current is derived . . ."

"Do you mean you are running the radio off *gravity?* Getting electricity for nothing?"

"Yes . . . really, I should say no. It is not like that . . ."

"It sure looks like that!" Charlie was excited now, crouching half across the table so he could look into the cigar box. "I may not know anything about electronics but in economics we learn a lot about power sources. Couldn't this gadget of yours be developed to generate electricity at little or no cost?"

"No, not at once, this is just a first attempt . . ."

"But it *could* eventually and that means—"

Sam thought that the young man had suddenly become sick. His face, just inches away, became shades lighter as the blood drained from it, his eyes were staring in horror as he slowly dropped back and down into his seat. Before Sam could ask him what was the matter a grating voice bellowed through the room.

"Anyone here seen a boy by name of Charlie Wright? C'mon now, speak up, ain't no one gonna get hurt for tellin' me the truth."

"Holy Jesus . . ." Charlie whispered, sinking deeper in the seat. Brinkley stamped into the bar, hand resting on his gun butt, squinting around in the darkness. No one answered him.

"Anybody try to hide him gonna be in trouble!" he shouted angrily. "I'm gonna find that black granny dodger!"

He started toward the rear of the room and Charlie, with his airline bag in one hand, vaulted the back of the booth and crashed against the rear door.

"Come back here, you son of a bitch!"

The table rocked when Charlie's flying heel caught it

and the cigar box slid off to the floor. Heavy boots thundered and the door squealed open and Charlie pushed out through it. Sam bent over to retrieve the box.

"I'll kill yuh, so help me!"

The circuit hadn't been damaged; Sam sighed in relief and stood, the tinny music between his fingers.

He may have heard the first shot but he could not have heard the second because the .38 slug caught him in the back of the head and killed him instantly. He crumpled to the floor.

Patrolman Marger ran in from the patrol car outside, his gun ready, and saw Brinkley come back into the room through the door in the rear.

"He got away, damn it, got clear away."

"What happened here?" Marger asked, slipping his gun back into the holster and looking down at the slight, crumpled body at his feet.

"I dunno. He must have jumped up in the way when I let fly at the other one what was running away. Must be another one of them commonists anyway, he was sittin' at the same table."

"There's gonna be trouble about this . . ."

"Why trouble?" Brinkley asked indignantly. "It's just anutha ol' dead nigger . . ."

One of his boots was on the cigar box and it crumpled and fractured when he turned away.

THE GREATEST CAR IN THE WORLD

Ernest Haroway's nerve was beginning to fail and he clasped his hands together to stop their shaking. What had seemed such a wonderful idea back in Detroit had become strange and frightening now that he was in Italy—and actually on the grounds of the Castello Prestezza itself. He controlled an involuntary shiver as his gaze rose up the gray and age-seared walls of the castle to the grayer and even more ancient palisade of the Dolomite Alps that loomed behind. The courtyard held a hushed and almost sacred stillness, broken only by the rustle of pine needles brushed by the late afternoon breeze, and the tacking of the cooling engine of his rented car. His throat was dry and the palms of his hands were wet. He had to do it!

With a convulsive motion he threw the door open and forced himself out of the car, stopping only long enough to grab up his briefcase before he crunched across the gravel toward the stone-framed and iron-bound portal of the castle.

There was no sign of bell or knocker on the dark wood of the door, but set into the stone at one side was a carved bronze gorgon's head, now green with age, with a rounded knob over its mouth. Haroway tugged at this knob and, with a grating squeal, it reluctantly came out about a foot on the end of the iron rod, then spasmodically returned to its original position when he released it. Whatever annunciatory mechanism it operated appeared to be functioning because within a minute there came a dreadful rattling from behind the door and it swung slowly open. A tall, sallow-faced man in servant's livery stared down the impressive length of his nose at the visitor, his eyes making a precise—and unimpressed—sweep the length of Haroway's charcoal gray, drip-dry, summer-weight suit, before fixing on his worried face.

"Sissignore?" he said through cold, suspicious lips.

"Buon giorno . . ." Haroway answered, thereby exhausting his complete Italian vocabulary. "I would like to see Mr. Bellini."

"The Maestro sees no one," the servant said in perfect English with a marked Oxford accent. He stepped back and began to close the door.

"Wait!" Haroway said, but the door continued to swing shut. In desperation he put his foot in the opening, a maneuver that had served him well during a brief indenture as a salesman while in college, but was totally unsuited to this type of architecture. Instead of bounding back, as the lightweight apartment doors had done, the monstrous portal closed irresistibly, warping the thin sole of his shoe and crushing his foot so tightly that the bones grated together. Haroway screamed shrilly and threw his weight against the door, which ponderously stopped, then reversed itself. The servant raised one eyebrow in quizzical condemnation of his actions.

"I'm sorry . . ." Haroway gasped, "but my foot. You were breaking all the bones. It is very important that I see Mr. Bellini, the Maestro. If you won't admit me you must take this to him." He dug into his jacket pocket while he eased his weight off the injured foot. The message had been prepared in advance in case there were any trouble in gaining admittance, and he handed it over to the servant, who reluctantly accepted it. This time the great door closed completely and Haroway hobbled over to one of the stone lions that flanked the steps and sat on its back to ease his throbbing foot. The pain died away slowly and a quarter of an hour passed before the door opened again.

"Come with me," the servant said. Was it possible that his voice was just a shade warmer? Haroway could feel his pulse beating in his throat as he entered the building. He was in—inside the Castello Prestezza!

The interior was dark and in his elated state he noticed no details, though he had a vague impression of carved wood, beamed ceilings, suits of armor, and pieces of furniture as bulky as freight cars. With uneven step he followed his guide through one chamber after another until they came to a room where tall, mullioned windows opened onto the garden. A girl stood in front of a window holding his note disdainfully by the edge, as though it were a soiled Kleenex she was about to discard.

"What do you want here?" she asked, the cold tones so unsuited to the velvet warmth of her voice.

At any other time Haroway would have taken a greater interest in this delightful example of female construction, but now, incredible as it seemed, he looked upon her only as an undesired interference. The jet-dark tresses dropping to the creamy tan of her shoulders were just hair. The ripeness of her bosom swelling above the square neck of her dress was another barrier placed in his way, while the pouting loveliness of her lips spoke only words that barred him from Bellini.

"It is no business of yours what I want here," he snapped. "I will tell that to the Maestro."

"The Maestro is a sick man and sees no one," she answered, her voice just as imperious as his. "We can have no one disturbing him." She dangled the card like a dead mouse. "What does this message mean— Unfinished business from Le Mans 1910?"

"That business is none of your business, Miss . . . ?"

"I am Signorina Bellini."

"Miss Signorina . . ."

"*Signorina* is the Italian word for 'Miss.' "

"Sorry. Miss Bellini. What I have to say is only for the ears of the Maestro himself." He took a firmer grip on the handle of his briefcase. "Now—will you take my message to him?"

"No!"

"*Chi è?*" a deep voice rumbled from the direction of the ceiling and the girl went white and clutched the note to her breast.

"He's heard . . . !" she gasped.

The apparently deific voice grumbled again and the girl answered it in staccato Italian, and appeared to be talking either to heaven or to a corner of the ceiling. After some blinking Haroway could make out a loudspeaker suspended from the crenelated molding with what appeared to be a microphone hanging next to it. Then the conversation terminated in what could only have been a command and the girl lowered her head.

"That was . . . he . . . him?" Haroway asked in a hushed voice. She only nodded her head and turned to the window until she could speak again.

"He wants to see you—and the doctor has expressly forbidden visitors." She swung about to face him and the impact of emotion in those large and tear-dampened eyes was so great that it cut through his indifference instantly. "Won't you leave—please? He's not to be excited."

"I would like to help you, but . . . I just can't, I've waited too long for this chance. But I promise you that I won't get him excited; I'll do my best, really I will."

She sighed tremulously and lowered her head again, turning. "Come with me," she said and started toward the door.

Haroway did not feel the pain of his injured foot, for in truth he felt scarcely anything as he stumbled after her as through a sea of cotton wool. His senses were suspended as though, unbelieving, they could not accept the fact that a lifetime ambition was being realized at last. One final door swung open and he could see the bulky figure swaddled in blankets and seated in a wheelchair—a chance ray of sunlight fell from the window and struck a reflection from his mane of white hair, a halo of light that would not have surprised Haroway if it had been real. He could only stand, petrified and speechless, while the girl went over and silently handed the Maestro his note.

"What does this mean?" the old man asked, waving the card at him. "There was only one piece of unfinished business at Le Mans that year and it is too late now to start a lawsuit or anything like that. What do you want?" He frowned at Haroway and the effort wrinkled a network of fine furrows into the mahogany skin.

"N-nothing like that," Haroway stammered, then took a deep breath and grabbed hold of himself. "I of course wasn't there; I hadn't even been born yet—" he fought down an impulse to giggle hysterically. "But my father has told me about it, many times, so I almost feel as if I had seen the race myself. When that eleven-litre FIAT brushed against your thirteen-hundred twenty-seven c.c. Type Thirteen and turned it over, what a horrible moment that must have been! But your driver, Fettuccine, was thrown clear and it was only when the radiator cap flew off and into the crowd . . ."

"The cap—I knew it!" the Maestro said, and pounded on the arm of the wheelchair. "It had to be that, there was no other unfinished business at Le Mans!"

"Grandfather, please!" the girl begged as she stroked his hand. "You promised not to!" she said, glaring at Haroway.

"I'm sorry, I didn't mean to. Anyway, there's nothing to get excited about, my father was the one who was hit on the head by the radiator cap."

"Aha—the mysterious wounded man, found at last."

"He wasn't really hurt; it was a very small fracture and he was out of bed inside of a month. And he still held onto the radiator cap—his greatest treasure. He had no money; he had worked his way to Europe just to see Le Mans, and he was treated in a charity hospital, that is why you never discovered him, though I know you tried very hard to find the man who had been injured."

"It was a mystery, many saw him fall—yet later there was no trace."

"Well Dad always was shy; he couldn't possibly consider talking to a great man like you. When he recovered he managed to make his way back to the United States and life was different for him after that. He always said that he had sown his wild oats and he was satisfied. When he met Mom and they married he worked in a filling station; then, finally, he saved enough to buy in and that was all he ever did—but he was always a happy man. He had the radiator cap sealed inside a glass case and framed and hung over the fireplace, and it's the earliest thing I remember, and him telling me about it. I grew up with that cap, Mr. Bellini, and it would be no lie to say that it shaped my whole life. I loved cars and I studied them and went to school nights and right now I'm an automotive engineer and there has never been anything else I have ever wanted in the whole world. Outside of meeting you, that is. Then Dad died last year and his last words were 'Take it back, son. It don't rightly belong to us and I knew it would have to go back someday, but couldn't bear to do it, not in my lifetime. That's your job, son, what you have to do. Take it back to the man that rightly owns it."

Haroway had his briefcase open and fumbled through it and extracted an object wrapped in many layers of polythene. One by one, with light, reverent touch, he unwrapped them until the old radiator cap was revealed, dented and scratched but polished like a jewel. He held it out to the Maestro who took and turned it over, squinting at it.

"A nice piece of brass," he said, then handed it back. "Keep it."

"Thank you," Haroway said in a humble voice as he carefully rewrapped it and slid it gently back into the briefcase. "Thank you, too, for your courtesy in receiving me." He locked the case and picked it up. "I'll not disturb you anymore—but, if you would permit, there is just one question I would like to ask before I go."

"What is that?" the Maestro asked distractedly, looking out the window and seeing only Le Mans in the year 1910. If it hadn't been for that hulking FIAT his Type Thirteen should have won. With the overhead camshaft they were getting 3,000 r.p.m. . . .

"It's something that has bothered me for years. Do you think that if it hadn't been for the accident that the Type Thirteen would have placed first? After all, with your new overhead camshaft you should have been getting 3,000 r.p.m. . . ."

"*Dio mio!*" the Maestro gasped. "You read my mind—those were my very thoughts!"

"Not really mind reading, sir, just a lifetime of study. I have had one hobby, one possessing enthusiasm and interest, the Bellini automobiles and the Bellini genius."

"A healthy hobby for a young man, most of the new generation are spineless wonders who think that a vehicle with an automatic gearshift is really a *car!* Stay a moment; you will have a glass of wine with me. Have you met my granddaughter, Vergine, the apple of an old man's eye even though she is very strict with me." She glared at him and he laughed heartily. "Don't scowl so, my blossom, it puts ugly lines upon your face. Instead bring a bottle of the '47 Valpolicella and some glasses, we shall have a little holiday today."

They drank and talked and the talk was only of

cars—Bellini cars, which they both agreed were the only fit cars to discuss. The afternoon faded and at dinner time an invitation was forced upon the not-reluctant Haroway and the talk continued; worm and wheel steering with the spaghetti, semicentrifugal, wet multiplate clutches with the meat, and banana-shaped tappets with the dessert. It was a highly satisfactory meal.

"There you see the proof," Haroway said, scratching a last number at the end of a row of equations that stretched across the white surface of the linen tablecloth. "When you developed your sixteen-valve engine for the Type Twenty-two with four valves per cylinder you developed higher scavenging pressure with the smaller valves—this *proves* it! Did you work out these equations first?"

"No. I leave it for others to prove. I *knew* what would happen, a matter of intuition you might call it."

"Not intuition—*genius!*"

Bellini nodded his great, gray head, accepting his due.

"What do you think I have been doing the past ten years?" he asked.

"Nothing. You retired to this castle after having given more to the automotive world than any other man."

"That is true. But, though I did retire, I have kept a small workshop here, for tinkering, working out ideas, an old man's hobby. I have constructed a car—"

Haroway went white, half rising to his feet, a convulsive movement of his hand sending one of the crystal wine glasses crashing to the floor: he was not aware of it.

"Car . . . new car . . ." was all he could gasp.

"I thought you might be a little interested," the Maestro said with an impish grin. "Perhaps you would like to see it?"

"Grandfather, no!" Vergine broke in. She had sat silently through the meal since the conversation seemed to be doing the Maestro no harm, mellowing his usually spiky mood, but this was too much. "The exertion, and the excitement, the doctor forbade you to go near the car for at least two weeks more . . ."

"Silence!" he roared. "This is my house and I am Bellini. No fat oaf of an overpaid quack tells me what to do in my own house." His temper changed and he patted her hand. "My darling, you must forgive an old man his moods. I have only a few laps left of the race of life and my magneto is failing and my oil pressure is low. Allow me a few moments of pleasure before I pull into the pit for the last time. You must have seen how different Haroway is from the other young men, for, even though he labors in the satanic mills of manufacture of Detroit iron, his heart is pure. I think he must be the last of a vanishing breed. He came here offering—not asking—expecting nothing. He shall see the car."

"What is it called?" Haroway asked in a hushed voice.

"The Type Ninety-nine."

"A beautiful name."

Haroway pushed the wheelchair and Vergine led the way to the elevator, which hummed down its shaft to the garage and workshop concealed beneath the castle. When the door opened Haroway had to hold onto the wheelchair for support or he would have fallen.

There was the car.

It was a moment of pure joy, the high point of his life. He did not realize that tears of unalloyed happiness were running down his face as he stumbled across the spotless concrete floor.

This was frozen motion. The silver form of the Type 99 was poised like a captive thunderbolt, yearning to leap forward and span the world. The body was simplicity itself, its curve as pure and lovely as that of a woman's breast. And under that glistening hood and concealed beneath the perfection of the body Haroway knew there were hidden even greater wonders.

"You installed . . . mechanical improvements?" he asked hesitantly.

"A few," the Maestro admitted. "The brakes, I have never given much attention before to the brakes."

"With good reason—did you not say yourself that a Bellini car is designed to go, not to stop?"

"I did. But the world changes and the roads are more crowded now. I have turned my attention to the brakes and devised a wholly new system of braking. Foolproof, nonfade, nongrab, impossible to lock, just what you imagine a Bellini brake should be."

"And the system is . . . ?"

"Magnetostriction."

"Of course! But no one ever thought of it before."

"Naturally. A laboratory phenomenon where the application of magnetism changes the dimensions of a ferromagnetic substance. It makes a good brake. And then I was so tired of the devil's dance of the piston engine. I decided a new principle was needed. The Type Ninety-nine is powered by a free-piston turbine."

"But—that's impossible! The two can't be combined."

"Impossible for others, not for Bellini. Another problem that has been eliminated is unsprung weight, this car has *no* unsprung weight."

"That's imposs . . ."

The Maestro smiled and nodded, accepting his accolade.

"There are a few other small items, of course. A nickel-cadmium battery that cannot wear out or be discharged completely. An all-aluminum body, rustproof and easy to repair, that sort of thing."

Haroway let his fingers caress the steering wheel. "You owe this car to the world."

"I had not thought of producing it. It is just an old man's toy."

"No, it is more than that. It is a return to the purity of the vintage motorcar, a machine that will take the world by storm. Just the way it is, the perfect car, the finest car in the world. You have patented all the modifications and inventions?"

"Bellini has been accused of a number of things, but never of having been born yesterday."

"Then let me take the car back with me to the United States! There are enough true car lovers in my firm, I only have to show them the Type Ninety-nine to convince them. We'll manufacture a limited number, loving care, hand labor, perfection . . ."

"I don't know," the Maestro said, then gasped and clutched at the arm of the chair, his face growing white with pain. "My medicine, quickly, Vergine." She ran for the bottle while he held tightly to his chest, speaking only with difficulty.

"It is a sign, Haroway, a greater power than I has decided. My work is done. The car is finished—and so am I. Take it, bring it to the world . . ."

He finished with a tired mumble and barely roused enough to sip the medicine his granddaughter brought to him. The noble head was hanging tiredly when she wheeled him away. After the doors of the elevator had shut behind them Haroway turned back to the car.

Joy!

A button on the wall swung open the garage door and a spray of windblown rain speckled the floor. The rented car could stay here; the firm could pick it up tomorrow, because tonight he was driving a Bellini! The car door opened to a touch and he slid into the comforting embrace of the leather driver's seat. He switched on the ignition, then smiled when he found out there was no starting button. Of course, Bellini had always disdained electric starters. A single pull on the crank was enough to start any Bellini car. Now the system had been refined to the utmost and a tiny, two-inch miniature crank handle protruded from the dashboard. He flipped it with his fingertips and the perfectly balanced engine roared into throbbing life. Through the wheel he could feel the vibrating power of the engine, not the mechanical hammer of an ugly machine but a muted rumble like the purr of a giant cat. With the ease of a hot knife cutting butter it slipped into first gear and when he touched the throttle the silver machine threw itself out into the night like an unleashed rocket.

Zero to a hundred miles an hour took four seconds because he was not yet used to the divine machine and was hesitant with the gas. Immense tunnels of light were cut through the rain-swept night by the searchlight-bright headlights. And, though there was no cover over the open car, he was perfectly dry as an ingeniously designed curtain of air rushed above him and shielded him from the rain. The road was a nightmare of hairpin turns but he laughed aloud as he snaked through them, since the steering was only one turn from lock to lock and as positive in response as though the car were running on rails.

There had never been a car like this in the history of the world. He sang as he drove, hurling his happiness into the sky. A new day was coming for the motoring world, the day of the Type 99. And they would all be manufactured with the same loving care that the master had lavished on this prototype, he would see to that.

Of course there would have to be one or two very minor modifications—like the battery. Nickel-cadmium was out, they had a contract with their lead-acid battery suppliers and you can't break a contract like that. And the aluminum body—good enough in theory, but you needed special dies to press it and they had stockpiled steel sheet that had to be used, and anyway the dealers would howl because the aluminum bodies would never rust or wear out and no one would trade in for a newer model. Then the engine would have to be considered: they would modify one of their stock engines. It was all right to say that here was a new principle, but they were tooled up to make a different kind of engine and you don't throw away a couple of million dollars worth of machine tools.

Anyway, a few changes under the hood didn't matter, the body would be the same. He glanced back happily at the car as he swung into the illuminated highway. Well, almost the same. You couldn't change a market overnight and there was something pretty European about the lines. Probably need fins to sell the U. S. market, fins were coming back big.

With a giant's roar from the exhaust he passed a clutch of sports cars as though they were standing still and swung out into a long bend of the road. The rain was clearing and on a ridge high above he could see the outlines of the Castello Prestezza and he waved his hand in a warrior's salute.

"Thank you, Bellini!" he shouted into the wind. "Thank you!"

That was the best part, the important part for him.

Not only would he be making the finest car in the world, but he would be making the old man's dream come true!

THE FINAL BATTLE

In the evening, after the dinner things have been cleared away, there is nothing we children enjoy more than sitting around the fireplace while Father tells us a story.

You may say that sounds foolish, or old-fashioned, with all the modern forms of entertainment, and if you say that you will forgive me if I smile indulgently?

I am eighteen and, in most other ways, I have put childish things behind me. But Father is an orator and his voice weaves a magic spell that still binds me, and, in all truth, I like it that way. Even though we won the War we lost a great deal in the process and it is a harsh and cruel world out there. I'm going to stay young just as long as I can.

"Tell us about the final battle," that is what the children usually say, and that is the story he usually tells. It is a frightening story, even though we know that it is all over now, but there is nothing like a good shiver up and down your spine before you go to sleep.

Father takes his beer, sips it slowly, then flicks the bits of foam from his moustache with his finger. That's the signal that he is going to begin.

"War is hell, and don't you forget it," he says, and the two youngest titter because they would have their mouths washed out with soap if *they* said the word.

"War is hell, it always has been, and the only reason I tell you this story is because I do not want you ever to forget that. We've fought the final battle of the last war, and a lot of good men died to win it, and now that it is over I want you always to remember that. If they had any reason for dying it was so that you could live. And never, ever, have to fight a war again.

"Firstly, abandon the idea that there is something ennobling or wonderful about battle. There is not. That is a myth that has been a long time dying and it probably dates from prehistory when war was hand-to-hand single combat, fought at the cave door as a man defended his home from the stranger. Those days are long past, and what was good for the individual can mean death for a civilized community. It meant death for *them,* didn't it?"

Father's big, serious eyes dart around the circle of listening faces, but no one will meet his gaze. For some reason *we* feel guilty, although most of us have been born since the War.

"We've won the War, but it is not really won if we do not learn a lesson from it. The other side might have discovered the Ultimate Weapon first, and if they had we are the ones who would be dead and vanished, and you must never forget that. Just a chance of history saved our culture and destroyed theirs. If this accident of fate can have any meaning for us, it must be that we learn a little humility. We are not gods and we are not perfect—and we must abandon warfare as the way to settle mankind's differences. I was there and I helped to kill them and I know what I am talking about."

After this comes the moment we are expecting and we all hold our breaths, waiting.

"Here it is," Father says, standing and reaching high up on the wall. "This is it, the weapon that rains death from a distance and is the Ultimate Weapon."

Father brandishes the bow over his head and is a dramatic figure in the firelight, his shadow stretching across the cave and up the wall. Even the smallest baby stops scratching for fleas under its fur wrapping and watches, gape-mouthed.

"The man with the club or the stone knife or the spear cannot stand before the bow. We've won our war and we must use this weapon only for peace, to kill the elk and the mammoth. This is our future."

He smiles as he hangs the bow carefully back on its peg.

"The waging of war is too terrible now. The era of perpetual peace has begun."

THE POWERS OF OBSERVATION

It's just a matter of native ability. I've had the same training as a lot of other guys, and if I remember things better or can jump faster than most of them, maybe that's the reason why I'm out here in no-man's-land where East brushes West and why they're behind desks in Washington.

One of the first things I was ever taught by the Department was to look out for the unusual. I whispered a soft word of thanks to my instructors as I watched this big, blond, Apollo type walk down the beach.

His feet sank into the sand!

Yes they did, and don't go telling me that that doesn't mean anything. The sand on the Makarska beach is like the sand on any other beach on the Yugoslavian coast, firm and compact. You can make footsteps in it—but not *that* deep.

All right, go ahead and laugh if you want to, but don't forget what I told you about my training, so just for the moment take my word about this. These footprints were unusual. I was sitting up and looking out to sea when he went by, and I didn't move my head to look at him. But, since I was wearing sunglasses, I followed him with my eyes, head dead center all the time. He was an absolutely normal guy; blond, about six foot, wearing blue nylon bathing trunks and sporting an appendectomy scar and a scowl. You see a million like him on every beach in the world every summer. But not with that kind of footprints.

Look, don't laugh, I asked you not to. I'll explain in a second. I let him walk on by and turn into the hotel, and while he was doing it I was standing up, and as soon as he was out of sight I was walking back the way he had come, toward this old woman who was selling *razniči* from a little stall. Sure I could have done it simpler, I was almost certain at the time that I wasn't under observation—but that's the point. I could have been. Unless people know better, if you act innocent—you are innocent. Act innocent all the time and etc. all the time. Pure as Lifebuoy, that's me. I went and had some *razniči,* my fourth portion for the day. Not that I like the things, but the stall made a good cover, an excuse for random action.

"Jedan," I said, and held up one finger in case my American accent obscured my tiny command of Serbo-Croatian. She bobbed her head and pulled a wood splint off the bed of charcoal and used her big carving knife to push the pieces of roasted meat from the splint onto the plate with the raw onion. Not a very complicated dish, but you get used to it after a while. To all appearances I was watching her carefully and digging out my money, but all I was really interested in were those footprints. I could see twelve of them from where I was standing, twelve that I was completely certain of, and while the food was being slowly dished out, and the battered aluminum dinar coins counted, two of them were obliterated by other bathers. I did a quick estimate of the elapsed time and the footprints destroyed and came up with an extrapolated life of six minutes for the remaining footsteps. Or three minutes with a one hundred-percent safety margin, which is the way I like to operate when I can. Good enough. I took my change, chewed the last gristly bit, and strolled back down the beach counting the coins.

Was it chance my course paralleled the remaining three footprints? Was it chance I walked at the same speed as the blond stranger? Was it chance that built the atom bomb?

My right foot came down in line with—and a few inches away from—a right footprint, and as my foot came up I dropped the coins. It took me exactly three point eight seconds to pick up the coins, and while picking them up I put my index finger into the blond man's heelprint and into my own. That's all. It was a risk to take, if anyone were watching, but calculated risks are part of this business.

I didn't smile and I didn't alter my walking pace, I just

jiggled my change and went back and sat down on my towel again.

That was outside. Inside it was Mardi Gras, Fourth of July, rockets and cherry bombs and ticker tape from the windows.

It was childishly simple. I'm five ten and weigh one eighty and I hit my foot into the sand in the same place and at the same speed and in the same way the blond had done. I could be off in my figure for the compressibility of the sand, but only by a small percentage, and I assumed it was displaced at a predictable rate on a sine curve; and I wasn't off at all in my measurement of the depth of the two impressions, so, plus or minus five percent for error, that six-foot-tall joker weighed in the neighborhood of four hundred and twelve pounds.

Jackpot!

Time for action. And thought. I could do both at the same time. He had gone into the hotel; I would go into the hotel. The Jadran was big, new, and international and almost everyone on this chunk of beach was staying there. As I picked up my towel and trudged slowly toward it I put the brain box into gear and thought of the next step. Communication and report, the answer came back instantly. The Department would be very interested in what I had discovered, and once I had relieved myself of the information I would be a free agent again and could look into the matter further. It should not be hard to find the heavyweight blond if he were registered at the hotel.

After the hot sunlight the lobby was dim, and apparently empty except for a fat German couple who were either asleep or dead in the overstuffed chairs. As I passed I looked into the bar and it was empty too, except for the bartender, Petar, who was polishing glasses listlessly. I turned in without breaking step, as though I had been headed here all the time and had not just decided at that instant to go in. The opportunity was too good to miss since Petar was my eyes and ears in this hotel—and well paid for the services.

"*Buon giorno,*" I said. "*Guten Tag,*" he sighed back. Petar comes from the island of Cres, which belonged to the Austrians until 1918 and then the Italians until 1945. He grew up with both languages as well as the native Serbo-Croatian. With this background he had picked up English and a little French and was in great demand as a bartender in the coastal hotels with their international clientele. He was also underpaid and undertipped and very happy to see my spanking-new greenbacks.

"Let me have a *pivo*," I said, and he took a bottle of East German dark beer out of the freezer. I climbed onto a stool and when he poured it out our heads were close together. "For ten bucks," I said, "the name and room number of a man, blond, six feet tall who wears blue swim trunks and has an appendectomy scar."

"How much is six feet?"

"One hundred and eighty-two centimeters," I flashed right back.

"Oh, him. A Russian by the name of Alexei Svirsky. Room one forty-six. He has a Bulgarian passport but he drives in a Tatra with Polish number plates. Who else but a Russian?"

"Who but." I knocked back the beer, and the tattered thousand-dinar bill I slipped him had a crisp sawbuck folded underneath it. The change came back, though the ten spot didn't, and I left a tip and headed for the door, but I wheeled around before I had gone two steps. I caught the trace of a vanishing smile on Petar's usually hounddog chops.

"For ten bucks more," I said, letting the palmed bill project a bit from under my hand on the bar top, "how much is Tovarich Svirsky paying you to report if anyone asks questions about him?"

"Five thousand dinar, cheapskate bum. Not him, his friends. He don't talk much."

"Here's ten thousand and another five when you tell me they asked and you told them there were no questions."

A slow nod, the bills shuffled and changed hands, and I left. My flanks guarded. I was very free with Uncle's money, but dinar aren't worth very much in any case. I went to my room, locked the door, tested to see if the place had been bugged since I left—it had not—then leaned out the open window. The pink concrete wall dropped six stories to a desolate patio floored with hard-tramped dirt and a few patches of yellowed grass. A row of dead plants leaned against one wall and four empty beer kegs baked and drew flies in the sun. There was no one in sight, nor were there any bugs on the wall outside my room. I sat down in the chair facing my window and the row of windows in the other wing of the hotel.

"How do you read me?" I said in a low voice.

Across the way a curtain was closed, then opened again. It was next to an open window.

"I've spotted a suspect. He may not be the one we were told to look out for, but there is strong evidence for believing that he is. Bulgarian passport but could be Russian. Name of Alexei Svirsky in Room one forty-six, and he weighs four hundred and twelve pounds. At a rough estimate." The curtain twitched an interrogative—"repeat."

"That's right. Four hundred and twelve pounds. I'm going to investigate."

As soon as I finished talking I turned away so that I wouldn't see the frantic jiggle of the curtain. I liked this setup: I didn't have to take any backtalk. The agent over there had a parabolic dish and a directional microphone. He could pick up a whisper in this room. But he couldn't talk to me.

While I was showering the phone rang but I ignored it. I could have been out, right? Moving a little faster now I pulled on slacks and a sport shirt and put on my sneakers with the ridged soles. There was no one around when I went out into the hall and down the stairs to the third floor, where, defying all logic, I knew Room one forty-six was located. Since I had passed on my old information it was time to gather some new. I found the room and knocked on the door.

Brash, perhaps, but a way to get results. I would mumble something about wrong room and get a closer look at Svirsky and the layout of his room. If my visit worried him and he ran, we would find out things; if he stayed, we would find some facts as well.

No one answered the door. I knocked again and leaned against the panel to listen. No shower, no voices, nothing. A little calculated risk was in order. The tooled-steel picklock worked as fast as a key would in this primitive lock, perhaps faster. I stepped in and closed the door behind me. The room was empty.

My bird had flown. There were still marks on the bed-cover where a suitcase had lain while it was being packed. The door of the big wooden wardrobe stood open, and if one of the coathangers had been swinging I would not have been surprised. It had all happened very quickly and efficiently. Nothing remained to mark Mr. Svirsky's visit. I went into the bath. The sink was dry, as was the shower, the towels folded neatly on the racks, threadbare but clean. Everything *too* clean and spotless, because I knew the chambermaids weren't that efficient. And Svirsky had been staying here some days—so this was positive information. There was even a trace of dust in the sink. I rubbed at it with my finger just as the hall door opened.

Just a crack, a couple of inches, then it closed again. But it was open long enough—and wide enough—to roll in a hand grenade.

As it bounced toward me I recognized the type (XII), place of manufacture (Plzn), and fuse time (three seconds). Even before this last fact had impressed itself I had jumped backwards, slammed the door, and collapsed inside the shower stall. Fast thinking and fast reflexes—that's a combination that can't be beat. I hoped, as I hunkered down with my arms clasped over my head.

It made a good deal of noise when it exploded.

The bathroom door blew in, fragments of grenade thudded into the wall above me and the mirror crashed in bursting shards to the floor. One steaming hunk of iron was imbedded in the tile about six inches in front of my nose. This was the closest piece, and it was close enough, thank you. I did not wait to examine it but was on my feet while the explosion still echoed, jumping over the remains of the destroyed bathroom door. Speed was the most important thing now because I didn't want to be found in this room. Diving through the still-roiling cloud of smoke I pulled open the tottering door—it collapsed at my feet—and made it into the hall. I could hear shouts and doors opening, but no one was in sight yet. The stairwell was five paces away; I got there without being seen and started up. Fleury was waiting on the landing above.

"Svirsky has cleared out," I told him. "He moved out fast and left someone behind to roll a grenade in on top of me." There were the sounds of running feet and shouts of multilingual amazement from the hall below. "That means they were tipped off about me, so I am forced to admit that my informant, Petar the bartender, is a double agent."

"I know. He was the one who threw the grenade into the room. We have him in the truck and are going to question him under scopolamine before we send him home. But I doubt if we'll learn anything; he's just small fry."

"What about Svirsky?"

"That's what I came to tell you. Our road watcher at Zadvarje, the next town, reports that a big Tatra with Polish plates just belted through there like a bomb, heading north towards Split. Two men in the front and one in the back. They were going too fast to make out anything more."

"Well that's more than enough. I'll take the jeep and go after them. Now that we have made contact we can't lose it."

Fleury chewed the inside of his lip worriedly. "I really don't know, it's a risk . . ."

"Crossing the street is a risk these days. Who do we have north of here that can head them off?"

"Just team Able Dog in Rijeka."

"That's pretty far away. Tell them to head south on the coastal highway, and if the Tatra doesn't turn off we'll have it trapped between us. We'll get a closer look at Tovarich Svirsky yet."

Five minutes later I was on the road north, tooling the jeep around the tight turns of the twisting highway. It wasn't really a jeep, but a Toyota land cruiser, with four-wheel drive, rugged and powerful. A Japanese car with Austrian plates and an American driver. We were about as international as the other side. I put my foot to the floor and hoped the driver of the Tatra would remember what the roads inland were like.

Yugoslavia is shaped like a right hand, palm up, with the Adriatic Sea all along the bottom edge, running along the side of the hand and the little finger. The coastal highway, what the locals call the *Magistrale,* runs all the way along the shore. I was on this highway now, about the base of the pinky, heading north toward the fingertip—where I hoped the other car was heading. That would be the fastest and easiest way to get out of the country, because Rijeka is up there at the end of the little finger and a good road turns east from there to Zagreb—on the top joint of the middle finger—and then on to Hungary at the tip of the index finger.

There was another way to get there that I hoped the comrades would not consider. The Velebit Mountains come right down to the coastline here, rugged and steep, and are crossed by the oldest and worst roads in the world. There are only a few of these goat tracks, all in terrible condition, and a car going this way could be easily followed and headed off. I was sure the driver of the Tatra knew this as well as I did and would make the correct decision.

I drove. The Toyota whined up to over eighty in the straight and skidded broadside around the turns. I passed a loafing Alfa-Romeo with Milan plates, on a turn, and the driver shook his fist out the window and blared his highway horn at me. Split was right ahead and I worked my way through the traffic as fast as I could without attracting the attention of the *milicija*. There was no sign of a black Tatra, though I kept my eyes open. When I passed the turnoff to Sinj I tried to ignore it. Although it was a good road for about fifty miles it degenerated into a bumpy cow path in the hills. I knew that and I hoped that the Tatra driver did as well. Once past Split I opened her up again and hoped that I was following a car—not just a hunch.

At Zadar I saw them. The highway makes a long swing to the right here, bypassing the city, and there is a big Jugopetrol gas station right in the middle of the curve. When I spotted the station far ahead, the Tatra was leaping out of it like a great black bug. They had stopped to fill their tank, or wash their hands, and given me enough time to catch up and get them in sight. I whistled as I belted around the turn and into the straight stretch that led to the Maslenica Bridge. There were a number of alternative plans and I was musing over them, deciding which was best, when we came up to the bridge and my right front tire blew out.

Since I was doing seventy at the time it was just a matter of good reflexes, good brakes—and luck. I twisted and skidded all over the road, and if there had been any traffic I would have had it right then. But the vanishing Tatra was the only other car around, and after some fancy work on the shoulder, two fence posts, and a cloud of dust, I slid up to the guard rail at the bridge plaza and bucked to a stop.

Blow out? Now that I had a moment to think I ran the old memory reel back and thought about that puff of smoke from the rear window of the Tatra just before the tire blew. Either this was a remarkable coincidence—or they had a gunport back there and someone was a very good shot with a hand pistol. I don't believe in coincidences.

For just about two seconds I thought about this and admired the view of harsh stone running down to the blue water of the arm of the sea below, and the bright orange bridge leaping over to the limestone cliff on the far side. Very dramatic. I was completely alone and the only sounds were the vanishing hum of the Tatra and the click of my hot engine. Then I unpried my fingers from the steering wheel and dug out the jack.

If they ever have a Toyota tire changing championship I'll place in the money. I threw the tools in the back, kicked her to life, and went after the comrades, more anxious than ever to take a closer look at the frightened Svirsky. The road along here is like nothing else on earth —in fact the landscape looks like the moon. Just rock, with sparse and dead-looking shrubs on it, falling straight to the sea, with the Adriatic Highway scratched along the face of the cliff. I concentrated on the driving, not on the view. I didn't see the Tatra again, though I did see Lukovo and Karlobag, jumbles of low, drab buildings, locked and tomblike under the heat of the afternoon sun. About five miles beyond Karlobag I saw a tan Mercedes coming from the other direction and I slammed on my brakes as it whistled by, burning rubber as well. Making a sharp U-turn I pulled up behind the Mercedes, which was stopped on the narrow shoulder next to the guard rail.

"Hi Able, Hi Dog," I said. "See any black Tatras lately?"

Martins, who had never smiled since I met him, shook his head in a lugubrious *no*. His partner, Baker, agreed.

"They have to have been here," I said, digging out my road map. "They were only a few miles ahead of me." I ran my finger along the map and sighed. "You're right. They're not. They turned off in Karlobag. They knew they were being tailed and even the dimmest of them could have figured out that there was a reception party ahead. Look."

I put my finger on the map and they looked. "A side road goes off into the mountains here, then over the top, where it joins up with a good road at Gospic. After that they have a straight run for the border. Once they are past the first stretch."

"The first part is marked in yellow," Martins said. "What does that mean?"

"I'm afraid to find out." The map, issued by *Turistički savez Jugoslavije,* was in Italian, and yellow roads were marked as being *Strada in macadam in cativo stato.* "In rough translation you could say unpaved and in lousy shape."

"That's bad," Martins said, looking like he was going to cry. "In Yugoslavia that is very bad."

"I'll give you a complete description of it when I make my report . . ."

"No," Martins said.

"Orders," Baker added. "We're supposed to take over the chase when we meet you. That came right down from the top."

"Not fair! I started this job and I should be left to finish it."

They shrugged, jumped into the Mercedes and charged off down the road. I climbed into the Toyota and followed them. So they could go first. But no one had said I couldn't be second.

In Karlobag a rusty sign labeled *Gospic 41* pointed up a hill at a cloud of dust. I hit the road and my brakes at the same time, then lurched forward in compound low. It was more of a quarry than a road, made up of rounded stones—some of them as big as table tops. I ground forward, dodging the worst ones, at five miles an hour. There was a loud explosion around the turn ahead. I hit the gas and bounced and skidded around it.

The Mercedes was off the road with its hood buried in

the ditch. Its front wheels were angled out as if they were very tired, and both fenders were peeled back like a pair of open tin cans. Things were still happening. A man in a dark suit stood up from behind a boulder on the far side of the road and leveled a long-barreled pistol. Before he could shoot, Martins, who had been driving, had his gun resting on the window ledge and fired just once. It was very dramatic. Black Suit screeched shrilly, threw his gun up in the air, spun about, and fell.

"Look after Baker," I shouted. "I'll take care of your friend."

I circled, fast and quiet, and came up behind the black-suited man, who was flat on the ground, trying to clamp his hand over his bleeding arm and wriggle over to his gun at the same time. "No seconds," I said, picking up the gun.

He rolled over and looked at me. *"Sveenyah . . ."* he growled.

"It is the same in every language," I told him, and pocketed the gun. "And who are you to call names? Do decent people travel around with land mines in their cars?" I left him that one to think about while I went back to help Martins. He had Baker laid out by the side of the road, the first aid kit open, and was smearing antiseptic on a bloody gash on the younger agent's forehead.

"Out cold," he said. "Breathing regular and it doesn't seem too bad—but you never know."

"Carry him back to the road—it's only a hundred yards—and flag down a car. There must be a doctor in this town. If not, there's a big hospital in Zadar. And if you remember it, you could send someone back to look at your target over there in the weeds. I'm going on to talk to Svirsky about the kind of friends he has."

I didn't give him time to argue, just started the Toyota and bounced away up the road. This was going to be a stern chase, where my four-wheel drive would finally come in handy. By missing the worst tombstones I could hold her at twenty, even twenty-five on some stretches. I was pretty sure the Tatra couldn't do this well, rugged as it is. Particularly when I saw it two turns above me on the snake-bended road.

All things considered, it was doing all right, bouncing

and swaying and throwing up a cloud of dust at all of ten miles an hour. These cars, which are never seen in the West, are the pride of the Skoda works. They're big and round and solid, only for high party officials and types like that. They are built and sprung to take punishment, too. With a high fin down the middle of their backs like a Flash Gordon rocket ship and three headlights in the front, they have more of a mad look than you would expect to find in this part of the world. Or maybe you would expect to. In any case, fin, headlights, and shocks weren't helping it to stay ahead. I was catching up slowly. We bounced and groaned and rattled around the bends and over the boulders, and I was less than two hundred yards behind him when I saw, around the next turn, a spire and a marker that might very well be the top of the hill. If he got there first, and onto a straight road, he might get away from me.

At this point the road headed away from the marker, went down and made a loop and came back on a higher level above the spot I was passing. A banked hillside separated the two stretches of road and I could see a beaten path where the pedestrians, goats, and dogs took a shortcut to save walking the long loop of road. Where four legs go, four wheels go. I pulled the wheel hard right and bounced through the ditch and into the dirt.

In all truth it was smoother and better than the road, although just a bit more angled. The engine growled, the tires spun and dug in, and we went straight up. I shouted *yippee* and held tight to the wheel.

When I came over the shoulder the Tatra had already rounded the turn and was bounding my way, its three eyes gleaming. For a churning moment the Toyota hung on the sharp lip, the front tires slipping on the smooth stones, until the back wheels dug in and shot us over the top.

Because the Tatra was about to pass me I did the only thing possible and ran full tilt into it.

I did manage to hit the hood so that the Tatra jarred sideways. There was a sound like an explosion in a garbage-can factory when we collided—then the Tatra nosed off the road and crashed into a well-placed pile of rocks. I braked, killed the engine, and jumped out at the same time, but Svirsky was faster. He had had the back door open even before the crash and had bounced out like an overweight gazelle. The driver was half slumped over the wheel, mumbling to himself as he tried to drag out another of those long-barreled pistols. I took it away from him and cracked him at the spot in the back of the neck that would put him to sleep for a while and keep him out of mischief. Then I followed Svirsky.

He had his head down and was pelting along the road like a runaway steam engine. But I just happen to be faster. When he reached the marker he turned off the road with me coming close behind him. I reached the high marker, passed it—then jumped back. The bullet tore a gouge from the stone just where I had been. Svirsky must have been the backseat marksman who had taken out my tire, and his eye was still good. Next to my head was an inscription, in German—something about this road's being dedicated to our noble Emperor, Franz-Josef. I believed it. And I bet it hadn't been touched since the emperor watched them roll the last boulder into place.

Keeping low, I ran around the other side of the commemoration plinth and saw Svirsky vanishing into a grove of pine trees. Great! If he had stayed on the road he could have kept me away with his deadly popgun. In the woods we were equal.

This was a northern forest, very much like the Alps. We had climbed high enough to leave the baked, subtropical coast behind and enter this pleasant green highland. Well, me Leatherstocking, him the moose. Or bear. I was going to do a little trapping. I could hear my prey crashing through the underbrush ahead, and I circled out to the side to swing around him, running low, silent, and fast.

My friend Svirsky was no Indian scout—or even a Boy Scout. He pushed those four hundred and twelve pounds through the woods like a tank, and I kept him in sonar contact at all times. When the crashing stopped I kept going until I had passed the spot where I had heard him last, then came silently back.

What a setup! He was bent over behind a tree, looking back the way he had come, the gun pointed and ready. I considered the best course, then decided that disarming him might be the wisest first step. I came up silently behind him.

"Can I borrow that, Comrade?" I said as I reached over and—with a good tug—pulled the gun out of his hands.

For all of his weight he had good reflexes. He swung at me and I had to jump aside to avoid getting slugged.

"Hands in the air, or *Hände hoch*, or whatever."

Svirsky ignored both me and the gun and, scowling terribly, he kept coming on in a wrestler's crouch, arms extended. I backed away.

"Someone can get hurt this way," I told him, "and the odds are that it's going to be you."

Still not a word, just that steady, machinelike advance.

"Don't say I didn't give fair warning. Stop, stop, stop —that's three times."

He completely ignored me so I shot him in the leg. The bullet ricocheted and screamed away and he kept coming. I could see the hole in his pants leg so I knew that I hadn't missed.

"All right, Iron Man," I said, aiming carefully, "let's see how good your joints are."

This time I aimed at his kneecap, with the same result. Nothing. I was backed up to a tree. I fired at the same spot once more before the bullets had any effect and the leg folded. But he was right on top of me then, coming down like a falling mountain. I couldn't get away in time and he hit me. I threw the gun as far away as I could before he closed those big hands on me.

Talk about strong, this joker had muscles of steel. I wriggled and twisted and kept moving, and I didn't try to hit him because I knew he had no nerves, no nerves at all. I twisted and pushed away, tearing most of my shirt off at the same time, and managed to get out of that mechanical bearhug.

Now it was my turn. I just climbed his back, locked my legs around his waist, and twisted his neck. He still hadn't said anything—I doubt if he could talk—but he thrashed his arms something terrible and tried to pull me off. He just couldn't reach me. I turned and turned and turned until he was glaring back at me over his right shoulder. And then I turned some more. He was facing straight backwards now, snapping his teeth at me. And I kept twisting. There was a sharp crack and his eyes closed and all the fight went out of him. I just turned some more until his head came off.

Of course there were a lot of trailing wires and piping and that kind of thing, but I pulled it all loose and put the decapitated head on the ground. Some of the wires sparked when they grounded.

Now I had to find out where the brain was. Just because a robot looks like a man there is no reason to assume that its brain is in its head. Svirsky may have thought with his stomach. I had to find out. Ever since we had heard the rumors that a humanoid robot was being field tested in Yugoslavia we had all been planning for this moment. Servo motors and power plants and hardware we knew about. But what kind of a brain were they using? We were going to find out. I pulled his shirt open—and they hadn't even bothered to put the plastic flesh back completely the last time they had serviced him. They must have been in a hurry to leave. A slap of skin was hanging loose just above his navel and I put my finger in and pulled. He peeled open just like a banana, showing a broad, metallic chest under the soft plastic. An access plate covered most of it, just as on an airplane's engine, with big slotted fasteners in the corners. I bent a ten dinar coin twisting them open, then pulled the plate off and threw it away.

Well, well, I smiled to myself, and even went so far as to rub my hands together. Motors, junction boards, power pack, and so forth, all feeding into a bundle of wires in a realistic location where the spinal cord should have been and heading up through the neck. Brain in head—and I had the head.

"Thank you, Comrade," I said, standing and dusting off my knees, "you have been very helpful. I'm going to borrow your shirt, because you tore mine, and take some pictures of your innards to make our engineers happy."

I removed the shirt from the headless torso and propped him up so that the sun shone in through the access port. Now, camera. I looked around carefully to be sure no one was in sight, then threw my torn shirt away.

"We have our secrets, too," I told him, but he didn't bother to answer.

I pushed with my thumbnail at the flesh over my sternum, then pulled with both hands until my skin stretched and parted. The lens of my chest camera protruded through the opening. "F two point five at a hundred twenty-fifth of a second," I estimated, correctly of course, then shot the pictures, clicking them off with a neural impulse to the actuator. I could easily hide the head in the Toyota and these photos would be all the detail we needed about the body. As there was no one else present I did not mind bragging aloud.

"Just like the space race, Comrade, neck and neck. And you went to the robot race the same way. Build strong, build for excess power, build your circuits double and treble in case of failure. That makes for a mighty heavy robot. Not even room left for speech circuits. While we build with micro- and micro-microminiaturization. Sophisticated circuitry. More goodness packed in the same package. And it works, too. When Washington heard you were going to be tested down here they couldn't resist field testing me at the same time."

I started back to the Toyota, then turned and waved good-bye with my free hand.

"If you have any doubt about which approach works the best," I called out cheerily, "just notice who is carrying whose head under his arm."

THE GHOUL SQUAD

1

"Look at them," Patrolman Charlie Vandeen said, jerking his thumb toward the gray vehicle parked on the other side of the road—then spitting in the same direction. "Just sitting there like vultures waiting for their pound of flesh. Vultures."

"The ITB have a job to do and they're doing it," Doc Hoyland said, pushing his fingers up under the back of the girl's jaw to find the fluttering pulse. "What did the ambulance say, Charlie? How long will they be?"

"Ten minutes more at least. They were way on the other side of town when the call came in." He looked down at the girl stretched out on the ground, at the thin limbs and cheap cotton dress, stained now with blood, and the bandage that covered her head like a turban. She was young, almost pretty: he turned quickly away and the gray bulk of the ITB wagon was still there, waiting.

"The ITB!" the young patrolman said loudly. "You know what people call them, Doc?"

"The Isoplastic Transplantation Bank . . ."

"No, you know what I mean. They call them the Ghoul Squad, and you know why."

"I know why, and I also know that is no way for a law officer to talk. They've got an important job to do." His voice changed as he pressed tighter, groping for the vanishing flutter of the pulse, weaker than a dying butterfly's wing. "She's not going to make it, Charlie, ambulance or no. She didn't bleed much but . . . half her brain is gone."

"There must be something you can do."

"Sorry, Charlie, not this time." He pulled the loose collar of her dress down and felt around the back of her neck. "Make a note for the record that she is not wearing a necklace and that there is no medallion."

"Are you sure?" the patrolman asked, flapping open his notebook. "Maybe it broke and fell down her dress . . ."

"Maybe it didn't. The chains are made of metal. Do *you* want to look?"

Although he was in his thirties Charlie was still young enough to blush. "Now don't go getting teed off at me, Doc; that was just for the record. We have to be sure."

"Well, I'm sure. Write that down, and the time, and what you see for yourself." He stood and waved his arm. The gray ITB truck rumbled to life and started over to them.

"What are you doing?"

"She's dead. No pulse, no respiration. Just as dead as the other two." He nodded toward the still smoking wreck of the pickup truck. "It just took a few minutes longer. She was really dead when they hit that tree, Charlie; there was never any chance."

Behind them the heavy tires braked to a stop and there was a slam as the rear door of the vehicle was thrown open. A man jumped down from the cab: the initials ITB in neat white letters were on the pocket of his gray uniform, the same gray as the truck. He spoke into a hand recorder as he approached.

"Eight April, 1976, on State Highway thirty-four, approximately seventeen miles west of Loganport, Georgia. Victim of an auto wreck, female, Caucasian, in her early twenties, cause of death . . ." he paused and looked up at Dr. Hoyland.

"Massive brain trauma. Almost the entire left frontal lobe of the cerebrum is gone."

As the driver came around the truck, snapping open a folding stretcher, the first ITB man turned to the patrolman.

"This is not a medical matter, Officer," he said, "and no longer a police concern. Thanks for your help."

Charlie had a quick temper. "Are you trying to get rid of me—"

Doc Hoyland took him by the arm and turned him away. "The answer is yes. You have no more business here now than you'd have in, well, in an operating theatre. These men have a job to do, and it must be done quickly."

Charlie's mind was made up for him as he heard the approaching wail of the ambulance. He went to flag it down and his back was turned as they bent and cut the clothes from the girl's body. Working quickly now they placed the corpse on the stretcher and drew a sheet of sterile plastic over it. A heavy curtain covered the open rear of the vehicle and they raised the bottom a bit to slide the stretcher under it.

When the patrolman turned back the men were already swinging the doors shut. At his feet was the blanket from the patrol car, speckled with the girl's blood and littered with the crumpled rags that had been her garments. A puff of vapor rose from a vent on top of the gray vehicle.

"Doc—what are they doing in there?"

The doctor was tired. He had had very little sleep the night before, and his temper was getting short.

"You know just as well as I do what they are doing," he snapped. "The ITB does a good job and a vital one. Only fools and crackpots think differently."

Charlie said *ghouls* as he started to the car to radio a report, but he didn't say it loud enough for the doc to hear.

2

This Christmas, in the year 1999, was really one for celebrations. Something about the new century being just a few days away seemed to excite everyone, that and the general prosperity and the tax cut that had been President Greenstein's holiday present to the entire country. What with Christmas falling on a Monday this year and the twenty-sixth now being an official holiday as well, the four-day weekend had been a very, very merry one. Someone had said that all the corn likker drunk in this one country would have floated a battleship and he was probably right—if it was a small battleship.

Sheriff Charlie Vandeen was nowhere near as tired as his deputies. In fact, he had to admit, he wasn't tired at all. He had not been home since the fire on the night of the twenty-third, but that didn't mean much. He had a cot in the room behind his office and he slept there, just as comfortably as in his bachelor apartment. His deputies knew where to find him in an emergency and that was good enough most of the time. Anyway, it hadn't been that kind of a holiday weekend—nothing really big, just a lot of everything little. Fires and drunks and fender benders, fights and noisy parties. Sheriff Charlie had had a good sleep. Now, showered and shaved and wearing a clean pressed uniform, he looked out at the foggy drab dawn of December twenty-six and wished the whole blamed holiday was over and people were back to work. The birthday of the Prince of Peace—the reverend had said that in church during the midnight service, when Charlie had looked in—which was his duty but not his pleasure. People sure had funny ideas how to celebrate that kind of birthday. He yawned and sipped at his steaming black coffee. Off in the distance there was a growing rumble; he looked at his watch. The morning hoverliner from the Bahamas, right on time.

Leaning back in the chair he unconsciously slipped into a familiar daydream. Something he always hoped to do. The drive to Macon, to the big hoverterminal on the Ocmulgee river outside the town. His bag whisked away, then up the gangplank into the arena-sized hoverliner. He'd be in the topside bar when they left; he'd seen enough pictures of it to know just what it would be like, looking down at the world rushing by. He'd have a mint julep first, to celebrate his leaving, then a Jamaica rum punch to celebrate the holiday ahead. He would sit up there, king of the castle, getting quietly wiped out while the pine slashes and swamps whooshed by below. Then the beach and the blue ocean and the golden islands ahead, the luxury hotel and the girls. In the daydream he always had a nice bronze tan when he walked out onto the beach, and he was a good bit younger. The gray streaks were gone from his hair and his gut was a good fifteen inches smaller. When the girls looked at him . . .

Through the reverie he was suddenly aware that the distant rumble had stopped. At the same moment the sky, above the low-hanging fog, lit up in a sudden rosy glare.

"Oh my God," he said, standing, unaware that the chair had fallen over backward and that the cup had dropped from his fingers, crashing on the floor. "Something's happened to it."

The hovercraft were foolproof, that's what they said, floating safely on a cushion of air, moving over land or water with equal ease. If, for some unaccountable reason, the engines should fail, they were supposed to simply sink down, to float or stand until they could move again. They were supposed to. Still, there had been some close calls—collisions and the like. When something the size of an ocean liner rushes along at over 150 miles an hour accidents are always possible. It looked as if the laws of chance had finally come up with a zero. Luck had run out. He reached for the phone.

While a deputy alerted the cars and the new ambulance service, and the fire department as well, Charlie verified the fact that a hoverliner, in his area, did not answer the call signal. He reported what he had seen and heard and hung up. He still hoped that his suspicions were wrong, but it was a very slight hope.

Jamming his hat onto his head he kicked into his high-heeled boots at the same time, then ran for the door, grabbing up his raincoat and gunbelt on the way. Unit three was parked at the curb outside and Ed Homer was dozing over the wheel. He jerked awake when the sheriff climbed in next to him: Homer hadn't heard the explosion. As they pulled away Charlie sent out an all-units alarm. There was no telling what they would find out there. He still hoped that he was wrong, but by now it was a mighty small hope.

"Do you think it hit in the swamp, Sheriff?" Ed asked, flooring the turbine and burning rubber down the highway.

"No, wasn't far enough west from what I could tell. And if it was we couldn't reach it in any case. I think it's still in the Cut."

"I'll take Johnson's road out, then the farm road along the Cut."

"Yeah," Charlie said, buckling on his gun.

It was full daylight now, watery and gray, but they still needed their lights for the patches of fog. They braked and broadsided into the side road and Ed touched the siren to pull over a lumbering milk truck on collection rounds. After that it was a straight run to the Cut, the broad highway through the pines that the hovercraft used. Grain couldn't be grown here, the downblast from the air cushion blew the kernels from their stalks, and grazing animals panicked when the big craft passed. A cash crop of grass for fodder was still possible, and the Cut was an immensely long meadow before it ran into the swamp. The cruiser bumped along the dirt track the harvesters used and there, dimly visible through the rising fog, was a boiling column of black smoke.

Ed Homer, wide-eyed, automatically took his foot from the accelerator as they came close. The hoverliner was gigantic in death, cracked open and smoking, tilted up where it had nosed into the trees after carving an immense raw furrow for five hundred yards through the field.

They drove slowly toward it, passing great tumbled sheets of black skirting torn from the bottom of the liner. People were climbing out of the wreck, lying in the grass, helping others to safety. The car braked to a stop, and when the turbine died they could hear the cries and shocked moans of pain.

"Get on the network and tell them exactly where we are," the sheriff said, throwing open the door. "Tell them we're going to need all the medical aid they can find. Fast. Then help to get those people clear."

He ran toward the wrecked liner, to the people sprawled on the ground. Some of them were burned and bloody, some of them obviously dead, some of them uninjured though still numb from the sudden shock. Two men in uniform carried a third uniformed man: his right leg hung at an impossible angle and there was a belt about his thigh that cut deeply into the flesh. He stifled a moan as they put him down before turning back to the wreck. The sheriff saw that the man was still conscious, though his skin was parchment white under the bruises and oil smears.

"Is there any chance of more fire or explosion?" he asked the man. At first the officer could only gasp, then gained a measure of control.

"Don't think so . . . automatic extinguishers kicked in when the engines blew. That's under control. But there is sure to be fuel leakage. No smoking, open fires, must tell them . . ."

"I'll see to that. Just take it easy, the ambulances are on the way."

"People inside . . ."

"We'll get them out."

The sheriff started toward the looming wreck, then stopped: the crew and male passengers seemed to be organized now. People were being helped to safety, even carried out on stretchers. It was more important for him to wait here for the assistance that would be arriving soon. He went back to the car and flicked the microphone switch from radio to bullhorn.

"May I have your attention please." He twisted the volume up full, and heads turned as his amplified voice rolled over them. "This is the sheriff speaking. I've called in medical aid and they'll be arriving at any moment now. I have been told that there may be fuel leakage and danger of fire—but there is no fire now. Do not smoke or light matches . . ."

There was a fluttering roar from behind him, growing louder. A copter, a big multirotor. This would be the ambulance people. Dust rolled out as the machine dropped close by and he put his back to it. When the blades slowed he turned to look. It was gray from nose to tail and Sheriff Charlie Vandeen felt that same hot needle of anger that had not lessened after all the years. He ran toward it as the entranceway dropped down.

"Get back inside, you're not wanted here," he called out to the two men who were hurrying down. They stopped, surprised.

"Who are you?" the first man asked. His hair, beneath his cap, was almost the same gray as the rest of his uniform.

"I'm the sheriff, you can read can't you?" He tapped at his badge, at the large clear letters, black on gold, but his fingers only brushed against the fabric of his shirt. Surprised, he looked down at the two empty holes in his pocket. When he had put on a clean uniform he hadn't changed his badge from the old one.

"You heard what I said," he called out to the men who had passed him while his attention had been on the missing badge. "The Ghoul Squad isn't needed here, not in my county."

The older man turned and looked back at him coldly.

"So you're *that* sheriff. I know about your county. Nevertheless we are doctors and since there are no other medical personnel present we intend to function in that capacity." He looked down at the sheriff's hand, which was rested on his pistol butt. "If you intend to fire upon us, you will have to shoot us in the back." He turned and both men started walking quickly toward the wreck.

The sheriff pulled his gun up a bit, then cursed and shoved it back. All right, fine, they were doctors. Let them act like doctors for once. That was okay by him.

Sirens sounded down the Cut and there were more copters coming in low over the trees. He saw Ed Homer helping a woman from the wreck and almost went to help, until he realized that he could do far more out here. Every kind of assistance would be arriving now and they would need organizing if they weren't to start falling over each other. The fire department pumper was bouncing across the field and they ought to get right up against the wreck to make sure there would be no fires. He ran out and waved to them.

Bit by bit organization replaced confusion. The unhurt passengers were guided from the area and the medical teams went to work on the wounded. Two local doctors had heard the call on the emergency network and had been temporarily drafted into the teams. One of them was old Doc Hoyland, in his seventies now and semiretired; he still rushed out like a firehorse when he heard the bell. He was needed today.

There was a growing row of figures covered with blankets that the sheriff glanced at once and turned away. When he did this he saw two men in gray carrying a stretcher toward their copter. In sudden anger he ran toward them, to the base of the entranceway.

"Is that man dead?" he asked, glancing quickly at the gaping mouth and staring, unmoving eyes. The lead stretcher bearer looked at the sheriff and almost smiled.

"Are you kidding? That's the only kind we ever go near. Now get out of the way——"

"Take him and put him over there with the other victims." Charlie touched the butt of his revolver, then grabbed it firmly. "That is an order."

The men hesitated, not knowing what to do, until the rear bearer said, "Set," and they put the stretcher on the ground. Charlie thumbed his pocket radio to life and talked quickly into it.

"Over there," the sheriff said, pointing. "I mean it and I'm playing no games." The men bent reluctantly just as the ITB doctor, whom the sheriff had first talked to, came hurrying up. There were two state troopers with him, both of whom the sheriff knew by sight. The sheriff spoke even as the doctor opened his mouth.

"You better load your ITB ghouls back aboard, Doc, and get out of here. There's going to be no hunting on my game preserve."

The doctor shook his head, almost sadly. "No, it is not going to be that way at all. I told you that we knew about you, Sheriff, and we have been avoiding trouble by keeping our units from entering your area of jurisdiction. We do not wish any public differences of opinion. However, this time we have no recourse but to make our position clear. The ITB is a Federal agency established by Federal law and no local authorities may interfere with it. We cannot create a precedent here. Therefore I must ask you to stand aside so that these men may pass."

"No!" the sheriff said hoarsely, color flooding his cheeks. "Not in my county . . ." He stepped back, his hand still on his gun as the two state troopers approached. The first one nodded at him.

"What the doctor says is right, Sheriff Vandeen. The law is on his side. Now you don't want to cause yourself any trouble."

"Step back!" the sheriff shouted, pulling at his gun, a loud roaring in his ears. Before it slid clear of the holster the two troopers were there, one on each side, holding him firmly. He struggled against them, gasping in air, trying to ignore the growing pain in his chest. Then he slumped forward suddenly, a dead weight.

The ITB doctor had the sheriff flat on the ground and was bent over him when Dr. Hoyland hurried up.

"What happened?" he asked, slipping his stethoscope from his pocket. He tore open the sheriff's shirt and put the pickup against his chest while he listened to the explanation. He opened his bag and gave the prone man a swift injection.

"Just what you might have expected," he said, struggling to stand. A trooper helped him to his feet. His face was as wrinkled as a hounddog's and had the same solemn expression. "But you can't talk to Charlie Vandeen. Angina pectoris, he's had it for years. Progressive heart deterioration. He's supposed to take it easy; you see how well he listens to me." A fine rain, no heavier than mist, was beginning to fall. The doctor drew his chin down inside his coat collar like an ancient turtle. "Get him out of this," he ordered.

The ITB men put the corpse aside and gently placed the sheriff on the stretcher. They carried it into their copter and the two doctors followed. Inside the body of the copter there was a narrow corridor formed by the curved inner wall and a partition of thin transparent plastic sheeting that stretched when they pressed against it. The sheriff was breathing hoarsely, laboriously, and his eyes were open now.

"I have been after him for the last five years to have a heart transplant. The one he's got is not strong enough to pump soda pop." Dr. Hoyland looked down, frowning grimly, while one of the stretcher bearers covered the sheriff with a blanket, up to the shoulders.

"He wouldn't do it?" the ITB doctor asked.

"No. Charlie has a thing about transplants and the ITB."

"I've noticed that," the doctor said, dryly. "Do you know why?"

The voices were distant, garbled hums to Charlie Vandeen, but his eyes worked well enough. He saw the two men carrying a stretcher with a man's body on it. They pushed it against the plastic wall, which parted like a great obscene mouth and drew it in. It was now in a small room walled with plastic where a man waited, dressed and masked in white. He stripped the body nude in an instant, then sprayed it all over with a nozzle hooked to a tank on the wall. Then, dripping with fluid, the corpse was rolled onto a plastic sheet and pushed through the other wall of this cell into the larger inside room.

Here the ghouls waited. Charlie did not want to look but he could not stop himself. On the table. A single practiced cut opened the body from sternum to pubis. Then dissection began. Something was removed from the gaping wound and, with long tongs, dropped into a container. Fumes rose up. Charlie moaned.

Dr. Hoyland nodded. "Of course I know why Charlie acts this way. It's no secret, it's just that nobody talks about it. He had a shock, right in the family, when he had just joined the state troopers. His kid sister, no more than sixteen as I remember, driving home from some school dance. Bunch of wiseacre kids, a hot rod, some moonshine, a crackup, you know the story."

The ITB doctor nodded, a little sadly. "Yes I do. And her medallion . . . ?"

"She left it home. She was wearing her first party dress, low neck, and it showed."

Through a thickening haze the sheriff saw something else, red and dripping, taken from the body and put into the box. He groaned aloud.

"It's going to take more than that shot," Dr. Hoyland said. "Do you have one of those new portable heart-lung machines here?"

"Yes, of course, I'll get it rigged." He pointed to his assistant who hurried away. "I cannot blame him for hating us, but it is all so useless. When the immune response was finally overcome in the seventies there were just no organs and limbs available for the people who desperately needed them. So the Congress passed the ITB law. If people do not want their bodies used to benefit others they simply wear a medallion that states this fact. They will never be touched. The act of not wearing a medallion means that the person involved is ready to donate whatever parts of his body may be needed. It's a fair law."

Dr. Hoyland grunted. "And a tricky one. People lose medallions or never get around to getting them and so forth."

"Here comes the machine now. It's a very just law. No one loses by it. Most of the religions—as well as the atheists—agree that the body is just so many inert chemicals after death. If these chemicals can benefit mankind, where is the argument? The ITB takes the bodies without medallions and removes the parts that we know are vitally needed. They are frozen in liquid nitrogen and go into banks all over the country. Do you think that the healthy kidney you just saw would be better utilized decomposing in the ground, rather than giving some dying citizen a long and happy life?"

"I'm not arguing. Just telling you how Charlie Vandeen feels. A man has a right to live or die his own way I've always believed."

Grunting with the effort he bent and readied the machine to preserve the life of the dying sheriff.

"N-no . . ." the sheriff gasped. "Take it away . . ."

"You're going to need this to save yourself, Charlie," Doc said softly. "This will keep you alive until we get you back to the hospital. We'll put a new pump in you then and you'll be good as new in a couple of weeks."

"No," the sheriff said, louder now. "Not to me you don't. I live and die with what God gave me. Do you think I could live with parts of someone else's body inside me. Why . . ." impotent tears filled his eyes, ". . . you might even be giving me my own little sister's heart."

"No, not after all these years, Charlie. But I understand." He waved away the man with the heart-lung machine. "I'm just trying to help you, not make you do any thing you think wrong."

There was no answer. The sheriff's eyes were open but he had stopped breathing. There, in those few seconds, he had passed that invisible dividing line. He was dead.

"He was a rough man but an honest one," Doc Hoyland said softly. "There have been a lot worse people in this world." He closed the dead man's eyes and climbed painfully to his feet. "I think we had better get back to work, Doctor. There are a lot more people out there who need us."

They had turned away when the ITB assistant called after them.

"Doctor, this man's not wearing a medallion."

Doc Hoyland nodded. "Not around his neck. He always said it might get torn off in an accident, must have told me a dozen times. Said that a sheriff always had his badge. You'll find the medallion soldered to the back of his badge."

They were at the exit before the assistant called after them again. "I'm sorry, doctor, but he doesn't seem to be wearing a badge. Are you sure about the medallion?"

"Of course, I'm sure." He turned shocked eyes to the ITB doctor, who waited stolidly beside him. "No—you can't! You know how he felt. I can send for his badge."

"The law states that the medallion must be somewhere on the person."

"I know the law, but you can't do this to him. Not Charlie. You can't . . ."

There were seconds of silence before the ITB doctor said: "What do you think?"

Then, gently, he led the old doctor out.

TOY SHOP

Because there were few adults in the crowd, and Colonel "Biff" Hawton stood over six feet tall, he could see every detail of the demonstration. The children—and most of the parents—gaped in wide-eyed wonder. Biff Hawton was too sophisticated to be awed. He stayed on because he wanted to find out what the trick was that made the gadget work.

"It's all explained right here in your instruction book," the demonstrator said, holding up a garishly printed booklet opened to a four-color diagram. "You all know how magnets pick up things and I bet you even know that the earth itself is one great big magnet—that's why compasses always point north. Well . . . the Atomic Wonder Space Wave Tapper hangs onto those space waves. Invisibly all about us, and even going right through us, are the magnetic waves of the earth. The Atomic Wonder rides these waves just the way a ship rides the waves in the ocean. Now watch . . ."

Every eye was on him as he put the gaudy model rocketship on top of the table and stepped back. It was made of stamped metal and seemed as incapable of flying as a can of ham—which it very much resembled. Neither wings, propellers, nor jets broke though the painted surface. It rested on three rubber wheels, and coming out through the bottom was a double strand of thin insulated wire. This white wire ran across the top of the black table and terminated in a control box in the demonstrator's hand. An indicator light, a switch, and a knob appeared to be the only controls.

"I turn on the power switch, sending a surge of current

to the wave receptors," he said. The switch clicked and
the light blinked on and off with a steady pulse. Then the
man began slowly to turn the knob. "A careful touch on
the wave generator is necessary as we are dealing with the
powers of the whole world here . . ."

A concerted *ahhh* swept through the crowd as the Space
Wave Tapper shivered a bit, then rose slowly into the air.
The demonstrator stepped back and the toy rose higher
and higher, bobbing gently on the invisible waves of
magnetic force that supported it. Ever so slowly the power
was reduced and it settled back to the table.

"Only seventeen dollars and ninety-five cents," the
young man said, putting a large price sign on the table.
"For the complete set of the Atomic Wonder, the Space
Tapper control box, battery, and instruction book . . ."

At the appearance of the price card the crowd broke up
noisily and the children rushed away toward the operating
model trains. The demonstrator's words were lost in their
noisy passage, and after a moment he sank into a gloomy
silence. He put the control box down, yawned, and sat on
the edge of the table. Colonel Hawton was the only one
left after the crowd had moved on.

"Could you tell me how this thing works?" the colonel
asked, coming forward. The demonstrator brightened up
and picked up one of the toys.

"Well, if you will look here, sir . . ." He opened the
hinged top, "You will see the space wave coils at each end
of the ship." With a pencil he pointed out the odd-shaped
plastic forms about an inch in diameter that had been
wound—apparently at random—with a few turns of cop-
per wire. Except for these coils the interior of the model
was empty. The coils were wired together and other wires
ran out through the hole in the bottom of the control box.
Biff Hawton turned a very quizzical eye on the gadget and
upon the demonstrator, who completely ignored this sign
of disbelief.

"Inside the control box is the battery," the young man
said, snapping it open and pointing to an ordinary
flashlight battery. "The current goes through the power
switch and power light to the wave generator . . ."

"What you mean to say," Biff broke in, "is that the juice
from this fifteen-cent battery goes through this cheap

rheostat to those meaningless coils in the model and absolutely nothing happens. Now tell me what really flies the thing. If I'm going to drop eighteen bucks for six bits' worth of tin, I want to know what I'm getting."

The demonstrator flushed. "I'm sorry sir," he stammered. "I wasn't trying to hide anything. Like any magic trick this one can't be really demonstrated until it has been purchased." He leaned forward and whispered confidentially. "I'll tell you what I'll do, though. This thing is way overpriced and hasn't been moving at all. The manager said I could let them go at three dollars if I could find any takers. If you want to buy it for that price . . ."

"Sold, my boy!" the colonel said, slamming three bills down on the table. "I'll give that much for it no matter *how* it works. The boys in the shop will get a kick out of it," he tapped the winged rocket on his chest. "Now *really*—what holds it up?"

The demonstrator looked around carefully, then pointed. "Strings!" he said. "Or rather a black thread. It runs from the top of the model, through a tiny loop in the ceiling, and back down to my hand tied to this ring on my finger. When I back up—the model rises. It's as simple as that."

"All good illusions are simple," the colonel grunted, tracing the black thread with his eye. "As long as there is plenty of flimflam to distract the viewer."

"If you don't have a black table, a black cloth will do," the young man said. "And the arch of a doorway is a good site; just see that the room in back is dark."

"Wrap it up, my boy, I wasn't born yesterday. I'm an old hand at this kind of thing."

Biff Hawton sprang it at the next Thursday night poker party. The gang were all missile men and they cheered and jeered as he hammed up the introduction.

"Let me copy the diagram, Biff; I could use some of those magnetic waves in the new bird!"

"Those flashlight batteries are cheaper than lox; this is the thing of the future!"

Only Teddy Kaner caught wise as the flight began. He was an amateur magician and spotted the gimmick at once. He kept silent with professional courtesy, and smiled ironically as the rest of the bunch grew silent one by one. The colonel was a good showman and he had set the scene well. He almost had them believing in the Space Wave Tapper before he was through. When the model had landed and he had switched it off he couldn't stop them from crowding around the table.

"A thread!" one of the engineers shouted, almost with relief, and they all laughed along with him.

"Too bad," the head project physicist said, "I was hoping that a little Space Wave Tapping could help us out. Let me try a flight with it."

"Teddy Kaner first," Biff announced. "He spotted it while you were all watching the flashing lights, only he didn't say anything."

Kaner slipped the ring with the black thread over his finger and started to step back.

"You have to turn the swtich on first," Biff said.

"I know," Kaner smiled. "But that's part of illusion— the spiel and the misdirection. I'm going to try this cold first, so I can get it moving up and down smoothly, then go through it with the whole works."

He moved his hand back smoothly, in a professional manner that drew no attention to it. The model lifted from the table—then crashed back down.

"The thread broke," Kaner said.

"You jerked it, instead of pulling smoothly," Biff said and knotted the broken thread. "Here let me show you how to do it."

The thread broke again when Biff tried it, which got a good laugh that made his collar a little warm. Someone mentioned the poker game.

This was the only time that poker was mentioned or even remembered that night. Because very soon after this they found that the thread would lift the model only when the switch was on and two and a half volts flowed through the joke coils. With the current turned off the model was too heavy to lift. The thread broke every time.

"I still think it's a screwy idea," the young man said. "One week getting fallen arches, demonstrating those toy ships for every brat within a thousand miles. Then selling the things for three bucks when they must have cost at least a hundred dollars apiece to make."

"But you *did* sell the ten of them to people who would be interested?" the older man asked.

"I think so; I caught a few air force officers and a colonel in missiles one day. Then there was one official I remembered from the Bureau of Standards. Luckily he didn't recognize me. Then those two professors you spotted from the university."

"Then the problem is out of our hands and into theirs. All we have to do now is sit back and wait for results."

"*What* results?! These people weren't interested when we were hammering on their doors with the proof. We've patented the coils and can prove to anyone that there is a reduction in weight around them when they are operating . . ."

"But a small reduction. And we don't know what is causing it. No one can be interested in a thing like that—a fractional weight decrease in a clumsy model, certainly not enough to lift the weight of the generator. No one wrapped up in massive fuel consumption, tons of lift, and such is going to have time to worry about a crackpot who thinks he has found a minor slip in Newton's laws."

"You think they will now?" the young man asked, cracking his knuckles impatiently.

"I *know* they will. The tensile strength of that thread is correctly adjusted to the weight of the model. The thread will break if you try to lift the model with it. Yet you can lift the model—after a small increment of its weight has been removed by the coils. This is going to bug these men. Nobody is going to ask them to solve the problem or concern themselves with it. But it will nag at them because they know this effect can't possibly exist. They'll see at once that the magnetic-wave theory is nonsense. Or perhaps true? We don't know. But they will all be thinking about it and worrying about it. Someone is going to experiment in his basement—just as a hobby, of course—to find the cause of the error. And he or someone else is going to find out what makes those coils work, or maybe a way to improve them!"

"And we have the patents . . ."

"Correct. They will be doing the research that will take them out of the massive-lift-propulsion business and into the field of pure space flight."

"And in doing so they will be making us rich—whenever the time comes to manufacture," the young man said cynically.

"We'll all be rich, son," the older man said, patting him on the shoulder. "Believe me, you're not going to recognize this old world ten years from now."

YOU MEN OF VIOLENCE

"I hate you, Raver," the captain shouted, his strained face just inches away, "and I know you must hate me too."

"Hate is too strong a word," the big man said quietly. "I think despise is much better."

There was no advance warning of the blow—the captain was too good a fighter for that—just the sudden jab that drove his fist into the other's stomach. Raver's only reaction was a slight and condescending grin. This infuriated the captain, who, though a head shorter than Raver, was still over six feet tall, and he expected some reaction other than scorn from the people he hit. In a blind rage he pummeled the other's unresisting form until Raver, leaking blood from nose and mouth, fell across the captain's desk, then slid limply to the floor.

"Get this carrion out," the captain ordered, rubbing at his bruised knuckles. "And clean up this filth." There were smears of blood across the surface of the desk, and everything on it had been swept to the floor when Raver fell. The Captain realized then that the blood was on him too and he dabbed at it distastefully with the kerchief from his sleeve. Still, there was some satisfaction in seeing the half-conscious bulk being carried from the room. "Now who is smiling," he shouted after them, then went out himself to wash and change.

Though the captain did not know it yet, he was the loser. From the moment he had boarded the prison ship two weeks earlier, Raver had been planning this encounter. All of his actions, his earlier confrontations with the captain, the hunger strike when the Phreban had been tortured—every bit of it had been planned with this final scene in mind. Raver had pushed the buttons, the captain had reacted as planned, and Raver had won. He leaned against the metal wall of his cell, clutching tightly the pencil-sized communicator that was concealed by his giant fist. When he had fallen across the desk he had palmed it. This was the reason for everything he had done.

Sighing heavily, Raver slumped to the floor and rolled over on his side. It was no accident that his back was to the glass eye of the monitor pickup, or that the barred door of his cell was in sight. Unobserved—and safe from surprise visitors—he allowed himself to smile as he set to work.

He had only a single tool, a nail which he had hidden in his boot sole and filed flat against the metal side of his bunk during the night. The squared tip now made a tiny screwdriver. His hand was a vise and his fingernails pliers and wrench. It was enough. There was no one still alive who knew Raver's real name, or anything about his earlier life before he went into crime and politics, and he certainly did not look like a typical microtechnician. Yet that was what he was, and a highly skilled one as well. The case of the communicator sprang open under his touch and the delicate leaves of the circuits fanned out. He went to work. There were only a few hours left to setdown and he needed all of them.

With infinite patience he disassembled the components, then rejoined them in new circuitry of his own design. He struck an arc from the tin battery to solder the connections, and could only hope that enough power remained to operate his device. It took a fraction over three hours to construct and for all of that time he lay still, with just his hands moving, an apparently unconscious bulk to the watchers in the prisoner control center. Only when the work was done did he permit himself to groan and stretch and to climb shakily to his feet. As he went to the barred door he stumbled, then held to the bars with one hand and pressed his forehead against the cool metal. In the preceding weeks he had stood this way for a good part of the waking day, so it was not considered unusual.

His right hand, shielded by his body, slid the wire probe into the opening of the lock while he slowly turned the knob on the variable capacitor.

An RF lock is theoretically pickproof, but that is just

theory. In practice a trained technician can cause the circuit to resonate at the keying frequency, which is what Raver did. A needle flickered briefly, and he made careful adjustments until it jumped across the dial and up against its stop. This was the operating frequency. Then he went to the sink and cleaned some of the blood from his face and at the same time reversed connections so that the probe became a transmitter. He was ready.

When the hooters sounded the two-minute warning for strapping down he paused for a moment at the door before going to his cot, which served double duty as an acceleration couch. The device had worked: he had felt the click as the electronic actuator had opened the lock. The door was open. Just before the landing rockets flared he pulled up his blanket and rolled over on his side to face the wall.

The rear jets kicked hard with 3 G's and the webbing of the bed stretched and creaked while Raver pulled himself slowly to his feet. This was the only time he could be sure that the guards in the prison control center would not be watching him. While they were fighting the deceleration he had to do what must be done. One shuffling step at a time he lurched his way across the cell, the muscles in his legs knotted and rock hard. The stool's three metal legs were welded to the floor and he had examined them and felt their thickness days earlier. Dropping heavily to his knees he seized the nearest leg in both hands, tensed his body—then pulled. The leg broke free with a sharp crack, and the other two were detached the same way. Then a slow shuffle back to the bed, onto which he put the stool and pulled the blanket over it. The ruse would not bear close examining, but it had to fool the watching guard on the screens for only a brief time. Back across the cell to the door, through it, close it, lock it, and down the passageway. His knees crumpled as more jets cut in for landing, 5 G's or more, but Raver continued on his hands and knees. He could move about safely only as long as the rockets were firing. When they cut out the crewmen and guards would unstrap and come out and he would be caught. Painfully and slowly he dragged himself across the passageway to the connecting ladder and began to work his way down.

The jets stopped when he was halfway to the bottom. He let go of the ladder and dropped.

Since the gravity on Houdt is less than Earth normal and because the fall was only fifteen feet, Raver did not injure himself, although he landed heavily. He rolled and crashed into the door with his shoulder as he came to his feet, throwing it open. Then he was through and running, heading for the space-suit locker. All around him he knew men were unstrapping themselves and rising, on their way. A door opened as he passed it and there was the sudden loud murmur of voices. Someone started through it—then turned to say something.

Raver hit the door of the locker, went through and closed it, and leaned against it.

There was no alarm.

Neither was there any time to waste. He took a long, shuddering breath, ignored his aching muscles, and turned to the racked space suits. The largest one, with its flexible fabric stretched to the limit, made a snug fit and he pulled it on. If he closed the helmet it would draw instant attention inside the ship—but if he left it open he would be instantly recognized. But the extra oxygen tanks would shield his face and serve a double purpose. The large refill tanks weighed over a hundred pounds apiece so he did not dare take more than two. Carrying more might draw attention. He had to go left so he swung the tanks onto his right shoulder and pushed the door open. When he went out he walked with his shoulder almost brushing the wall, and the tanks shielded his face from view.

Footsteps passed him, but he was not stopped. He went down two decks and saw the guard on the emergency airlock just as the alarms sounded. Raver walked on steadily, neither faster nor slower, though the guard jumped nervously and slipped his rifle from his shoulder and held it at port arms.

"What is it? What's happened?" he called to Raver, then turned to look down the connecting corridor. The pulsating hooters split the air. "Who are you?" the guard asked when Raver came closer. It was only then, far too late, that he tried to bring his rifle to bear.

Raver reached out with his free hand and took the man by the throat so he could not shout a warning, then pulled him close so he could not use the gun. One long finger moved up to the artery under the guard's ear and clamped down, cutting off the flow of blood to the brain. The man struggled helplessly for a few seconds, then slumped, unconscious. Raver was careful to lay him gently on the deck before he stripped him of weapon and munition pouches, slung the rifle over his shoulder and opened the airlock. There were shouts behind him as he closed and dogged it shut, but he ignored them.

"Get him," the captain ordered, his face suffused with blood. "Bring him back to me. Kill him only if you must, because I want to see him die. Do you understand?"

"Yes, sir," Lieutenant N'Ness said, keeping his face expressionless. "I'll need a squad of the most fit men to go with me."

"You have them. What do you plan to do?"

N'Ness snapped open a map and spread it on the desk. He was a career soldier and after this tour of field duty he was returning to staff college. He explained with professional brevity and clarity.

"The ship is here, near the base of the cliff, within the usual landing area. Raver can gain nothing by going toward the prison mines here—and in fact all the observers place him on an eighty-six-degree course toward the foothills here. This makes sense. The nearest mining settlement—other than the prison—is here, on the other side of the mountains. It is operated by Puliaans."

"The devil!"

"Exactly. If Raver reaches them they will give him sanctuary and there is nothing that we can do about it."

"I know what I would like to do . . ." the captain mumbled, clenching his fist.

"You're not the only one," Lieutenant N'Ness said. "But Puliaa has three times our population and five times our industrial capacity. There is nothing that we can do."

"Yet. Someday though . . ."

"To be sure. Meanwhile, the escaped prisoner is heading for sanctuary. He has taken two refill tanks in addition to the tank on his suit. This will give him enough oxygen to reach the Puliaan mine—but only by the most direct route. If he tries to hide or dodge about he will not make it in time. I intend to follow at once with the best men available, each carrying a single spare oxygen tank. We will be light and fast. We will capture him and return."

"Go, then. You have my instructions."

The squad had already suited up and N'Ness hurried to join them. In spite of the need for speed he checked every weapon, ammunition pouch, and oxygen tank before moving them out. Then they left on the double, across the plain and into the foothills, following directions radioed from the ship, heading for the spot where Raver had vanished from sight.

"I have it," N'Ness radioed back. "Dislodged stones, footprints, there is a clear trail here that I can follow. Next report in one hour." He led the squad into the mountains of Houdt.

Houdt. A ruined and gutted world with its atmosphere stripped away in some ancient cataclysm, its surface riven and its metallic core laid bare. There were heavy metals here for the taking, all the power metals that made a voyage across the light years possible. Since there was still more than enough for all, there was no competition and the planet's surface was dotted with mines, each maintained by a different world or syndicate. The best of them were robot operated, the worst of them manned by human slaves.

Raver had neither the temperament to be a slave nor a slave holder, yet there was no other choice on his world. He had gone into opposition to the established regime and it was remarkable that his opposition had lasted as many years as it had before he, inevitably, ended up on Houdt. Nor was he dead yet. Once over the mountains and down into the Puliaan settlement and he would be safe.

The oxygen tanks were slung on his back to free his arms, and he needed his arms on these steep slopes. As he pulled himself up the face of the fissured rock, it exploded silently next to him, boulders' dust and gravel billowing out. He felt the concussion through his fingertips and let go his hold and slid back down to the safety of the jagged rocks below. Looking through a fissure he saw his pursuers for the first time, kneeling in an ordered row as they fired. As soon as he vanished from sight they jumped to their feet and came on. Raver went on as well, taking a longer course, which would keep him out of their sights.

"We'll rest now," Lieutenant N'Ness ordered as the sun neared the horizon. His men dropped. The chase had begun soon after dawn and the days here were twenty standard hours long. They were in the far northern latitudes, where the axial tilt conspired to form a night less than three hours in length. N'Ness had considered pushing on through the darkness, but it would not be worthwhile. The climbing was almost impossible at night and his men were exhausted. They would sleep and catch the slave before another sunset.

"A two-man guard, one hour for each watch," he said. "Stack all the extra oxygen tanks here. In the morning we'll top our tanks and see how many of these we can leave behind."

Most of them were asleep before he finished talking. He kicked the nearest one awake to help him collect the tanks, then they sat, back to back, for the first watch.

The sunlight hit first on the highest peaks at dawn, but without an atmosphere to diffuse the light only the smallest, reflected part fell on the camp. The third watch, on the lieutenant's orders, was waking them up and they were just starting to stir when the night exploded.

It was light, flame, then darkness and the shouts of frightened men in the darkness. The lieutenant beat them into order and the arrival of full dawn showed them that their reserve store of oxygen had been destroyed.

Reconstructing what had happened was not hard. Raver must have crept close during the night, lain there, then walked in at dawn, just one more space-suited man. He had put a bomb of some kind in among the tanks, then escaped in the confusion following the blast. N'Ness had underestimated him.

"He will pay for it," the lieutenant said coldly. "He lost his lead by coming back to do this—and he will not regain it. Fall in and check tanks."

The spare oxygen cylinders were gone, but there was still some oxygen left in the suit tanks. With ruthless efficiency N'Ness bled these tanks into his, until his was full and the others close to empty. "Get back to the ship," he ordered. "As soon as you get past these last hills use your radio; you should be able to raise either the ship or the mine. Tell them to bring oxygen out to meet you in case you don't have enough to make it all the way. I'm going on and I'll bring the prisoner back. Report that to the captain. Now move out."

N'Ness did not watch them go, in fact he had already forgotten their existence. He was going to catch Raver. He was going to march him back at gunpoint. It would make the captain very happy and it would look very good on his record. He almost ran up the slope ahead.

The lieutenant was the lighter man, he was more lightly burdened, and he had the advantage of being the follower, not the pathfinder. Where Raver had worked his way around a difficult patch of broken rock, N'Ness went straight through, counting upon his speed and agility. He did not slow nor rest and his panting breath was echoed by the whine of the conditioning unit as it labored to remove the excess water vapor and heat. It was an insane chase, but as long as he did not slip or collapse from exhaustion it could have only one end.

Raver pulled himself up onto the broad ledge and through a gap in the rocks he could see the tall pithead workings of the Puliaan mines. He started forward when his radio crackled in his ear, and N'Ness's voice said, "Just hold it, right where you are." He stopped dead and looked slowly around.

Lieutenant N'Ness stood on the ledge above, pointing his energy rifle. "Turn around," N'Ness said, "and start right back where you came from." He waggled the muzzle of the gun in the correct direction.

"Thank you, no," Raver said, sitting down and slinging the oxygen tank to the ground. "I have no intention of returning, in spite of your invitation."

"Enough talk. You have ten seconds to start moving—before I pull this trigger."

"Pull and be damned. I die here or I die back there. What difference does that make to me?"

N'Ness had not expected this, and he had to think a moment before he answered. The steel edge of command was gone from his voice when he finally spoke. "You're a reasonable man, Raver. There's no reason to die out here, not when you can live and work . . ."

"Don't act stupid, the role doesn't become you. We

both know that mine slaves are there for life—and a short life at that. There'll be no more chances to escape. You're the paid killer. Shoot."

N'Ness estimated the reserves in his tank and the spare Raver carried and sat down himself. "You can leave out the insults," he said. "I may have killed men in the line of duty, but I've never tortured or butchered people the way your so-called Pacifist Party . . ."

"Stop," Raver ordered, lifting his head. "You're a victim of your own propaganda. It's all lies. We do not kill. Think for yourself, if you are able to. Have you ever seen any of the atrocities committed that you speak about? Other than by your own people, that is."

"I'm not here to argue with you . . ."

"Unsatisfactory, try again. Have you seen these things?"

"No, I haven't—but that's only because we shot first and fast before they could happen."

"Just as unsatisfactory, Lieutenant. You are avoiding the truth. You kill, we do not. That is the basic and important difference between us. You are the animal heritage of mankind, we are its future."

"Not so holy, please. You attacked the guard on the ship, and last night you tried to kill me and my men."

"That is not true. I do not kill. I rendered the guard unconscious and I used the guard's rifle and ammunition as a bomb to destroy your oxygen, to force you to turn back. Was anyone injured?"

"No, but . . ."

"*Yes*, but," Raver said loudly, jumping to his feet. "That is all the difference. Our aggressive traits brought us to the top of the animal kingdom, now we must renounce killing if we are to progress. We have this violence within us—I don't deny I have it myself—but what good is our intellect if we cannot control it? Any man can desire a woman he sees in the street or jewelry in a display window, yet only the sick men rape and steal. We all possess the capacity for violence. Only the sick man kills."

"Not sickness," N'Ness said, waggling the gun in Raver's direction. "Just good sense. This wins arguments. The sensible man knows he can't fight a gun, so he gets one himself and evens the score. That's something you people will never learn. We always win. We kill you."

"Yes, you kill us in great numbers, but you cannot win. You do not change a man's mind by eliminating him. What do you do when everyone is on the other side? Shoot them all? And after you have killed every man, woman, and child—what do you do with your world?"

"You're being stupid now. This has been tried before, and whenever the leaders are killed the mob does what it is told."

"Then there is something new come into the universe," Raver said quietly. "Perhaps it is the next development, homo superior, a mutation, men who are constitutionally unable to kill. This is not my theory, there have been scientific papers written on it . . ."

"All nonsense!"

"Not really. Look at what happened on Puliaa."

"Propaganda. The Pacifist Party there may be temporarily in power, but watch what happens at the first sign of trouble."

"They've had their trouble and they've weathered it well so far. And it is truth that a worldwide nonviolent rebellion put them into power. It it what everyone wanted."

"Lies!"

"I doubt it." Raver smiled. "You can't ignore the fact that the entire planet is now vegetarian. Something happened. Why don't you look into it before it is too late. I'm not the first one to believe that those who live by the sword die by it."

"That's enough talk," N'Ness said, standing. "You'll come back with me now."

"No."

"If you don't come I'll shoot you down, now, and send men for your body. You have no choice."

"Would you do that? Just pull the trigger and kill a man? Remove a life for no reason? I find it hard to imagine; I am incapable of such an evil act."

"It is not evil—and I have good reason. You are an enemy, I have orders . . ."

"Those are not reasons, just excuses. An animal kills to eat or in defense of its own life, or the lives of others. All else is corruption."

"One last warning," N'Ness said, aiming the gun steadily at the other's midriff. "Your arguments mean nothing. Come with me or I shoot you."

"Don't do this to yourself, Lieutenant. Here is a chance rarely offered to your kind. You can stop killing. You can go with me to Puliaa and discover what it is like not to be an animal. Don't you realize the rapist rapes himself? Who would want to live in the head of a rapist? So does the killer kill himself, and this is probably the only kind of killing a man of peace can understand. We do not like it, but by necessity we accept it. Only when your kind is gone can my kind make this galaxy the place it should be."

"You fool," the lieutenant shouted. "You're dying, not me. Your last chance."

"You kill yourself," Raver said calmly.

The lieutenant's lips pulled back from his teeth and he shouted with rage as he pulled the trigger.

The gun blew up, killing him instantly.

"I'm sorry," Raver said. "I tried to tell you. During the night I fixed your rifle to explode, as I did the other. I was hoping that you would come with me."

Head lowered with sorrow, Raver turned and walked toward the mine visible below.

"You of course realize, Mr. Lamb, that not one hunter has ever bagged a Venusian swamp-thing?" Godfrey Spingle spoke into the microphone, then shoved it toward the other man.

"Indeed I do. I've read all the records and studied all the reports. That is why I am here on Venus. I have been called the finest hunter in the world and, to be perfectly honest, I would rather enjoy being called the finest hunter in *two* worlds."

"Well, thank you, Mr. Lamb. And may the best wishes of the Intrasystem Broadcasting Company go with you, as well as all of the listening millions out there. This is Godfrey Spingle, in Muckcity, on Venus, signing off." He flipped the switch and stowed the mike back in the recorder case.

Behind them the shuttle rocket roared as it blasted up through the damp air and Lamb waited until the sound had died away before he spoke.

"If the interview is finished, I wonder if you would be kind enough to tell me which of these . . ." He pointed toward the ramshackle collection of tottering structures, ". . . is the hotel."

"None of them." Spingle picked up two of Lamb's bags. "It sank into the mud last week, but I have a cot for you in one of the warehouses."

"That's very kind of you," Lamb said, picking up the other two cases and staggering after his long-legged guide. "I hate to put you to any trouble."

"No trouble," Spingle said, unsuccessfully keeping a thin note of complaint out of his voice. "I used to run the hotel too before it went down. And I'm the customs officer and mailman. There's not much of a population in this place—or any damn reason why there should be."

Spingle was sorry for himself and angry at the injustice of the world. Here he was, six foot two, strong and handsome, and rotting away in this filthy hole. While Lamb, five foot four, round and fat, with bifocals was famous—as a hunter! No justice, no justice at all.

Lamb began rooting in his bags as soon as they were dropped onto the mildewed concrete floor. "I want to go out at once, shoot a swamp-thing before dark so I can get the morning rocket back. Would you be so kind as to tell the guide."

"I'm the guide." He had to control his sneer. "Aren't you being a little, well, optimistic about your chances. The swamp-things can swim, fly, walk, and swing from trees. They are wary, intelligent, and deadly. No one has ever shot one of them."

"I shall," Lamb said, taking a gray coverall from his bag and pulling it on. "Hunting is a science that I alone have mastered. I never fail. Hand me that head, please."

Wordlessly, Spingle passed over a large papier-mâché head that had white teeth and red eyes painted on it. Lamb slipped it over his own head, then pulled on gray gloves, followed by gray boots with white claws dangling from them.

"How do I look?" he asked.

"Like a fat swamp rat," Spingle blurted out.

"Fine." He took a gnarled stick from his bag and placed it between the jaws of the mask. "Lead the way, Mr. Spingle, if you please."

Spingle, at a complete loss for words, belted on his pistol and took the path into the swamp.

"I'll give you a one minute start," Lamb said as the last building vanished behind them in the mist, "then follow your footprints. Be careful, I understand these swamps are quite deadly."

"Deadly! That's an understatement. Take my advice, Lamb, and go back."

"Thank you, Mr. Spingle," the muffled voice said from inside the grotesque head, "but I shall proceed."

Spingle led the way; let the fool get eaten by the

swamp-things or any other local beasts. Once the idiot was gone his bags could be gone through and there should be something of value . . .

The unmistakable sound of a blaster echoed through the damp air and, after a moment's paralysis, Spingle ran back down the path with his own handgun ready.

It was not needed. Lamb sat on the rotting trunk of a fallen tree, the discarded mask-head beside him, mopping sweat from his face with a large bandanna. Beyond him, half in and half out of the jungle, was the hideous fang-toothed, claw-winged, poison-green corpse of a swamp-thing, frightful even in death.

"How . . . ?" Spingle gasped. "What . . . you . . . how?"

"A simple story," Lamb said, digging a camera from his pocket, "a discovery I made some years back. I found out that I was heavy of foot and bad of eye, an undistinguished tracker and an unaccomplished woodsman. Though I'm a damn fine shot; I pride myself on that. My ambition was to be a hunter, but I could never get close enough to my prey to get in a shot. So, with impeccable logic, I changed roles. After all—these beasts are born hunters and killers, so why should I compete on their terms? Instead I became prey and let the beasts stalk and attack me—to be killed themselves, of course. In the guise of the oryx, skin-draped and horn-headed, I have knelt by the stream and killed the swift leopard. As a very slow zebra I have bagged my share of lions. It is the same here. My research showed that the swamp-things live almost exclusively off of the giant swamp rat, *rattus venerius*. So I became a rat—with this result." He raised the camera and photographed the dead beast.

"Without a gun?"

Lamb pointed to the twisted stick, leaning now against the log, that he had carried in his rodent teeth. "That is a disguised blaster. These creatures would have recognized a gun at once."

Then the idea came to Spingle. The swamp-thing was dead and *he* had the gun—and the secret. Lamb would vanish in the swamp and he would be the finest hunter in the world. Two worlds. He raised his weapon.

"So long, sucker," he said. "Thanks for the tip."

Lamb only smiled and pressed the flash button on his

camera. The blaster, concealed inside, blew a neat hole through Spingle before he could press his own trigger. Lamb shook his head.

"People never listen. I'm fit prey for *all* hunters. Now, let me see, that makes my bag one swamp-thing—and thirteen, no, fourteen would-be assassins."

DOWN TO EARTH

"Gino . . . Gino . . . help me! For God's sake, do something!"

The tiny voice scratched in Gino Lombardi's earphone, weak against the background roar of solar interference. Gino lay flat in the lunar dust, half buried by the pumice-fine stuff, reaching far down into the cleft in the rock. Through the thick fabric of his suit he felt the edge crumbling and pulled hastily back. The dust and pieces of rock fell instantly, pulled down by the light lunar gravity and unimpeded by any trace of air. A fine mist of dust settled on Glazer's helmet below, partially obscuring his tortured face.

"Help me, Gino—get me out of here," he said, stretching his arm up over his head.

"No good—" Gino answered, putting as much of his weight onto the crumbling lip of rock as he dared, reaching far down. His hand was still a good yard short of the other's groping glove. "I can't reach you—and I've got nothing here I can let down for you to grab. I'm going back to the Bug."

"Don't leave . . ." Glazer called, but his voice was cut off as Gino slid back from the crevice and scrambled to his feet. Their tiny helmet radios did not have enough power to send a signal through the rock; they were good only for line-of-sight communication.

Gino ran as fast as he could, long gliding jumps one after the other back toward the Bug. It did look more like a bug here, a red beetle squatting on the lunar landscape, its four spidery support legs sunk into the dust. He cursed under his breath as he ran: what a hell of an ending for the

78

first moon flight! A good blast-off and a perfect orbit, the first two stages had dropped on time, the lunar orbit was right, the landing had been right—and ten minutes after they had walked out of the Bug Glazer had to fall into this crevice hidden under the powder dust. To come all this way—through all the multiple hazards of space—then to fall into a hole . . . There was just no justice.

At the base of the ship Gino flexed his legs and bounded high up toward the top section of the Bug, grabbing onto the bottom of the still-open door of the cabin. He had planned his moves while he ran—the magnetometer would be his best bet. Pulling it from the rack he yanked at its long cable until it came free in his hand, then turned back without wasting a second. It was a long leap back to the surface—in Earth gravitational terms—but he ignored the apparent danger and jumped, falling and rolling when he landed. The row of scuffled tracks stretched out toward the slash of the lunar crevice and he ran all the way, chest heaving in spite of the pure oxygen he was breathing. Throwing himself flat he skidded and wriggled like a snake, back to the crumbling lip.

"Get ready, Glazer," he shouted, his head ringing inside the helmet with the captive sound of his own voice. "Grab the cable . . ."

The crevice was empty. More of the soft rock had crumbled away and Glazer had fallen from sight.

For a long time Major Gino Lombardi lay there, flashing his light into the seemingly bottomless slash in the satellite's surface, calling on his radio with the power turned full on. His only answer was static, and gradually he became aware of the cold, from the eternally chilled rocks, that was seeping through the insulation of his suit. Glazer was gone, that was all there was to it.

After this Gino did everything that he was supposed to do in a methodical, disinterested way. He took rock samples, dust samples, meter readings, placed the recording instruments exactly as he had been shown, and fired the test shot in the drilled hole. Then he gathered the records from the instruments and when the next orbit of the Apollo spacecraft brought it overhead he turned on the cabin transmitter and sent up a call.

"Come in, Dan . . . Colonel Danton Coye, can you hear me . . . ?"

"Loud and clear," the speaker crackled. "Tell me, you guys, how does it feel to be walking on the moon?"

"Glazer is dead. I'm alone. I have all the data and photographs required. Permission requested to cut this stay shorter than planned. No need for a whole day down here."

For long seconds, there was a crackling silence, then Dan's voice came in, the same controlled Texas drawl.

"Roger, Gino—stand by for computer signal, I think we can meet in the next orbit."

The moon takeoff went as smoothly as the rehearsals had gone in the mock-up on Earth, and Gino was too busy doing double duty to have time to think about what had happened. He was strapped in when the computer radio signal fired the engines that burned down into the lower portion of the Bug and lifted the upper half free, blasting it up toward the rendezvous in space with the orbiting mother ship. The joined sections of the Apollo came into sight and Gino realized he would pass in front of it, going too fast: he made the course corrections with a sensation of deepest depression. The computer had not allowed for the reduced mass of the lunar rocket with only one passenger aboard. After this, matching orbits was not too difficult and minutes later Gino was crawling through the entrance of the command module and sealing it behind him. Dan Coye stayed at the controls, not saying anything until the cabin pressure had stabilized and they could remove their helmets.

"What happened down there, Gino?"

"An accident—a crack in the lunar surface, covered lightly, sealed over by dust. Glazer just . . . fell into the thing. That's all. I tried to get him out, I couldn't reach him. I went to the Bug for some wire, but when I came back he had fallen deeper . . . it was . . ."

Gino had his face buried in his hands, and even he didn't know if he was sobbing or just shaking with fatigue and strain.

"I'll tell you a secret, I'm not superstitious at all," Dan said, reaching deep into a zippered pocket of his pressure suit. "Everybody thinks I am, which just goes to show you how wrong everybody can be. Now I got this mascot, because all pilots are supposed to have mascots, and it makes good copy for the reporters when things are dull." He pulled the little black rubber doll from his pocket, made famous on millions of TV screens, and waved it at Gino. "Everybody know I always tote my little good-luck mascot with me, but nobody knows just what kind of good luck it has. Now *you* will find out, Major Gino Lombardi, and be privileged to share my luck. In the first place this bitty doll is not rubber, which might have a deleterious effect on the contents, but is constructed of a neutral plastic."

In spite of himself, Gino looked up as Dan grabbed the doll's head and screwed it back.

"Notice the wrist motion as I decapitate my friend, within whose bosom rests the best luck in the world, the kind that can only be brought to you by sour mash one-hundred-and-fifty proof bourbon. Have a slug." He reached across and handed the doll to Gino.

"Thanks, Dan." He raised the thing and squeezed, swallowing twice. He handed it back.

"Here's to a good pilot and a good joe, Eddie Glazer," Dan Coye said raising the flask, suddenly serious. "He wanted to get to the moon and he did. It belongs to him now, all of it, by right of occupation." He squeezed the doll dry and methodically screwed the head back on and replaced it in his pocket. "Now let's see what we can do about contacting control, putting them in the picture, and start cutting an orbit back toward Earth."

Gino turned the radio on but did not send out the call yet. While they had talked their orbit had carried them around to the other side of the moon and its bulk successfully blocked any radio communication with Earth. They hurtled their measured arc through the darkness and watched another sunrise over the sharp lunar peaks: then the great globe of the Earth swung into sight again. North America was clearly visible and there was no need to use repeater stations. Gino beamed the signal at Cape Kennedy and waited the two and a half seconds for his signal to be received and for the answer to come back the

480,000 miles from Earth. The seconds stretched on and on, and with a growing feeling of fear he watched the hand track slowly around the clock face.

"They don't answer . . ."

"Interference, sunspots . . . try them again," Dan said in a suddenly strained voice.

The control at Kennedy did not answer the next message, nor was there any response when they tried the emergency frequencies. They picked up some aircraft chatter on the higher frequencies, but no one noticed them or paid any attention to their repeated calls. They looked at the blue sphere of Earth, with horror now, and only after an hour of sweating strain would they admit that, for some unimaginable reason, they were cut off from all radio contact with it.

"Whatever happened, happened during our last orbit around the moon. I was in contact with them while you were matching orbits," Dan said, tapping the dial of the ammeter on the radio. "There couldn't be anything wrong . . . ?"

"Not at this end," Gino said grimly. "But something has happened down there."

"Could it be . . . a war?"

"It might be. But with *whom* and why? There's nothing unusual on the emergency frequencies and I don't think . . ."

"*Look!*" Dan shouted hoarsely, "The lights—where are the lights?"

In their last orbit the twinkling lights of the American cities had been seen clearly through their telescope. The entire continent was now black.

"Wait, see South America—the cities are lit up there, Gino. What could possibly have happened at home while we were in that orbit?"

"There's only one way to find out. We're going back. With or without any help from ground control."

They disconnected the lunar Bug and strapped into their acceleration couches in the command module while they fed data to the computer. Following its instructions they jockeyed the Apollo into the correct attitude for firing. Once more they orbited the airless satellite and at the correct instant the computer triggered the engines in the attached service module. They were heading home.

With all the negative factors taken into consideration, it was not that bad a landing. They hit the right continent and were only a few degrees off in latitude, though they entered the atmosphere earlier than they liked. Without ground control of any kind it was an almost miraculously good landing.

As the capsule screamed down through the thickening air its immense velocity was slowed and the airspeed began to indicate a reasonable figure. Far below, the ground was visible through rents in the cloud cover.

"Late afternoon," Gino said. "It will be dark soon after we hit the ground."

"At least it will still be light. We could have been landing in Peking at midnight, so let's hear no complaints. Stand by to let go the parachutes."

The capsule jumped twice as the immense chutes boomed open. They opened their face plates, safely back in the sea of air once more.

"Wonder what kind of reception we'll get?" Dan asked, rubbing the bristle on his big jaw.

With the sharp crack of split metal a row of holes appeared in the upper quadrant of the capsule: air whistled in, equalizing their lower pressure.

"Look!" Gino shouted, pointing at the dark shape that hurtled by outside. It was egg-shaped and stub-winged, black against the afternoon sun. Then it twisted over in a climbing turn and for a long moment its silver skin was visible to them as it arched over and came diving down. Back it came, growing instantly larger, red flames twinkling in its wing roots.

Gray haze cut off the sunlight as they fell into a cloud. Both men looked at each other: neither wanted to speak first.

"A jet," Gino finally said. "I never saw that type before."

"Neither did I—but there was something familiar — Look, you saw the wings didn't you? You saw . . . ?"

"If you mean did I see black crosses on the wings, yes I did, but I'm not going to admit it! Or I wouldn't if it wasn't for those new air-conditioning outlets that were just installed in our hull. Do you have any idea what it means?"

"None. But I don't think we'll be too long finding out. Get ready for the landing—just two thousand feet to go."

The jet did not reappear. They tightened their safety harnesses and braced themselves for the impact. It was a bumping crash and the capsule tilted up on its side, jarring them with vibration.

"Parachute jettisons," Dan Coye ordered. "We're being dragged."

Gino had hit the triggers even as Dan spoke. The lurching stopped and the capsule slowly righted itself.

"Fresh air," Dan said and blew the charges on the port. It sprang away and thudded to the ground. As they disconnected the multiple wires and clasps of their suits, hot, dry air poured in through the opening, bringing with it the dusty odor of the desert.

Dan raised his head and sniffed. "Smells like home. Let's get out of this tin box."

Colonel Danton Coye went first, as befitted the commander of the First American Earth-Moon Expedition. Major Gino Lombardi followed. They stood side by side silently, with the late afternoon sun glinting on their silver suits. Around them, to the limits of vison, stretched the thin tangle of grayish desert shrub, mesquite, cactus. Nothing broke the silence, nor was there any motion other than that caused by the breeze that was carrying away the cloud of dust stirred up by their landing.

"Smells good, smells like Texas," Dan said, sniffing.

"Smells awful, just makes me thirsty. But . . . Dan . . . what happened? First the radio contact, then that jet . . ."

"Look, our answer is coming from over there," the big officer said, pointing at a moving column of dust rolling in from the horizon. "No point in guessing, because we are going to find out in five minutes."

It was less than that. A large, sand-colored half-track roared up, followed by two armored cars. They braked to a halt in the immense cloud of their own dust. The half-track's door slammed open and a goggled man climbed down, brushing dirt from his tight black uniform.

"*Hände hoch!*" he ordered, waving their attention to

the leveled guns on the armored cars. "Hands up and keep them that way. You are my prisoners."

They slowly raised their arms as though hypnotized, taking in every detail of his uniform. The silver lightning bolts on the lapels, the high, peaked cap—the predatory eagle clasping a swastika.

"You're—you're a *German!*" Gino Lombardi gasped.

"Very observant," the officer observed humorlessly. "I am Hauptmann Langenscheidt. You are my prisoners. You will obey my orders. Get into the *Kraftwagen.*"

"Now just one minute," Dan protested. "I'm Colonel Coye, USAF, and I would like to know what is going on here . . ."

"Get in," the officer ordered. He did not change his tone of voice, but he did pull his long-barreled Luger from its holster and leveled it at them.

"Come on," Gino said, putting his hand on Dan's tense shoulder. "You outrank him, but he got there fustest with the mostest."

They climbed into the open back of the half-track and the captain sat down facing them. Two silent soldiers with leveled machine pistols sat behind their backs. The tracks clanked and they surged forward: stifling dust rose up around them.

Gino Lombardi had trouble accepting the reality of this. The moon flight, the landing, even Glazer's death he could accept; they were things that could be understood. But this . . . ? He looked at his watch, at the number twelve in the calendar opening.

"Just one question, Langenscheidt," he shouted above the roar of the engine. "Is today the twelfth of September?"

His only answer was a stiff nod.

"And the year—of course it is—1971?"

"Yes, of course. No more questions. You will talk to the *Oberst,* not to me."

They were silent after that, trying to keep the dust out of their eyes. A few minutes later they pulled aside and stopped while the long, heavy form of a tank transporter rumbled by them, going in the opposite direction. Evidently the Germans wanted the capsule as well as the men who had arrived in it. When the long vehicle had passed, the half-track ground forward again. It was growing dark when the shapes of two large tanks loomed up ahead, cannons following them as they bounced down the rutted track. Behind these sentries was a car park of other vehicles, tents, and the ruddy glow of gasoline fires burning in buckets of sand. The half-track stopped before the largest tent and at gunpoint the two astronauts were pushed through the entrance.

An officer, his back turned to them, sat writing at a field desk. He finished his work while they stood there, then folded some papers and put them into a case. He turned around, a lean man with burning eyes that he kept fastened on his prisoners while the captain made a report in rapid German.

"That is most interesting, Langenscheidt, but we must not keep our guests standing. Have the orderly bring some chairs. Gentlemen, permit me to introduce myself. I am Colonel Schneider, commander of the one-hundred-ninth Panzer division, which you have been kind enough to visit. Cigarette?"

The colonel's smile just touched the corners of his mouth, then instantly vanished. He handed over a flat package of Player's cigarettes to Gino, who automatically took them. As he shook one out he saw that they were made in England—but the label was printed in German.

"And I'm sure you would like a drink of whisky," Schneider said, flashing the artificial smile again. He placed a bottle of Ould Highlander on the table before them, close enough for Gino to read the label. There was a picture of the highlander himself, complete with bagpipes and kilt, but he was saying *Ich hätte gern etwas zu trinken WHISKEY!*

The orderly pushed a chair against the back of Gino's legs and he collapsed gratefully into it. He sipped from the glass when it was handed to him—it was good Scotch whisky. He drained it in a single swallow.

The orderly went out and the commanding officer settled back into his camp chair, also holding a large drink. The only reminder of their captivity was the silent form of the captain near the entrance, his hand resting on his holstered gun.

"A most interesting vehicle that you gentlemen arrived in. Our technical experts will of course examine it, but there is a question—"

"I am Colonel Danton Coye, United States Air Force, serial number . . ."

"Please, Colonel," Schneider interrupted. "We can dispense with the formalities . . ."

"Major Giovanni Lombardi, United States Air Force," Gino broke in, then added his serial number. The German colonel flickered his smile again and sipped from his drink.

"Do not take me for a fool," he said suddenly, and for the first time the cold authority in his voice matched his grim appearance. "You will talk for the Gestapo, so you might just as well talk to me. And enough of your childish games. I know there is no American Air Force, just your Army Air Corps, which has provided such fine targets for our fliers. Now—what were you doing in that device?"

"That is none of your business, Colonel," Dan snapped back in the same tones. "What I would like to know is, just what are German tanks doing in Texas?"

A roar of gunfire cut through his words, sounding not too far away. There were two heavy explosions and distant flames lit up the entrance to the tent. Captain Langenscheidt pulled his gun and rushed out of the tent while the others leaped to their feet. There was a muffled cry outside and a man stepped in, pointing a bulky, strange-looking pistol at them. He was dressed in stained khaki and his hands and face were painted black.

"*Verdamm* . . ." the colonel gasped and reached for his own gun: the newcomer's pistol jumped twice and emitted two sighing sounds. The Panzer officer clutched his stomach and doubled up on the floor.

"Don't just stand there gaping, boys," the intruder said, "get moving before anyone else wanders in here." He led the way from the tent and they followed.

They slipped behind a row of parked trucks and crouched there while a squad of scuttle-helmeted soldiers ran by them toward the hammering guns. A cannon began firing and the flames started to die down. Their guide leaned back and whispered.

"That's just a diversion—just six guys and a lot of noise—though they did get one of the fuel trucks. These krautheads are going to find it out pretty quickly and start heading back here on the double. So let's make tracks—*now!*"

He slipped from behind the trucks and the three of them ran into the darkness of the desert. After a few yards the astronauts were staggering, but they kept on until they almost fell into an arroyo where the black shape of a jeep was sitting. The motor started as they hauled themselves into it and, without lights, it ground up out of the arroyo, and bumped through the brush.

"You're lucky I saw you come down," their guide said from the front seat. "I'm Lieutenant Reeves."

"Colonel Coye—and this is Major Lombardi. We owe you a lot of thanks, Lieutenant. When those Germans grabbed us, we found it almost impossible to believe. Where did they come from?"

"Breakthrough, just yesterday, from the lines around Corpus. I been slipping along behind this divison with my patrol, keeping San Antone posted on their movements. That's how come I saw your ship, or whatever it is, dropping right down in front of their scouts. Stars and stripes all over it. I tried to reach you first, but had to turn back before their scout cars spotted me. But it worked out. We grabbed the tank carrier as soon as it got dark and two of my walking wounded are riding it back to Cotulla, where we got some armor and transport. I set the rest of the boys to pull that diversion and you know the results. You air corps jockeys ought to watch which way the wind is blowing or something, or you'll have all your fancy new gadgets falling into enemy hands."

"You said the Germans broke out of Corpus—Corpus Christi?" Dan asked. "What are they doing there—how long have they been there—or where did they come from in the first place?"

"You flyboys must sure be stationed in some hideaway spot," Reeves said, grunting as the jeep bounded over a ditch. "The landings on the Texas side of the Gulf were made over a month ago. We been holding them, but just barely. Now they're breaking out and we're managing to stay ahead of them." He stopped and thought for a moment. "Maybe I better not talk to you boys too much until we know just what you were doing there in the first place. Sit tight and we'll have you out of here inside of two hours."

The other jeep joined them soon after they hit a farm road and the lieutenant murmured into the field radio it carried. Then the two cars sped north, past a number of tank traps and gun emplacements and finally into the small town of Cotulla, straddling the highway south of San Antonio. They were led into the back of the local supermarket, where a command post had been set up. There were a lot of brass and armed guards about and a heavy-jawed one-star general behind the desk. The atmosphere and the stares were reminiscent in many ways of the German colonel's tent.

"Who are you two, what are you doing here—and what is that *thing* you rode down in?" the general asked in a no-nonsense voice.

Dan had a lot of questions he wanted to ask first, but he knew better than to argue with a general. He told about the moon flight, the loss of communication, and their return. Throughout the general looked at him steadily, nor did he change his expression. He did not say a word until Dan was finished. Then he spoke.

"Gentlemen, I don't know what to make of all your talk of rockets, moon shots, Russian sputniks, or the rest. Either you are both mad or I am, though I admit you have an impressive piece of hardware out on that tank carrier. I doubt if the Russians have time or resources now for rocketry, since they are slowly being pulverized and pushed back across Siberia. Every other country in Europe has fallen to the Nazis and they have brought their war to this hemisphere, have established bases in Central America, occupied Florida, and made more landings along the Gulf Coast. I can't pretend to understand what is happening here so I'm sending you off to the national capital in Denver in the morning."

In the plane next day, somewhere over the high peaks of the Rockies, they pieced together part of the puzzle. Lieutenant Reeves rode with them, ostensibly as a guide, but his pistol was handy and the holster flap loose.

"It's the same date and the same world that we left," Gino explained, "but some things are *different.* Too many things. It's all the same up to a point, then it changes radically. Reeves, didn't you tell me that President Roosevelt died during his first term?"

"Pneumonia, he never was too strong, died before he had finished a year in office. He had a lot of wild-sounding schemes but they didn't help. Vice-president Garner took over, but it didn't seem the same when John Nance said it as when Roosevelt had said it. Lots of fights, trouble in Congress, Depression got worse, and things didn't start getting better until about '36, when Landon was elected. There were still a lot of people out of work, but with the war starting in Europe they were buying lots of things from us: food, machines, even guns."

"Britain and the Allies, you mean?"

"I mean everybody, Germans too, though that made a lot of people here mad. But the policy was no-foreign-entanglements and do-business-with-anyone-who's-willing-to-pay. It wasn't until the invasion of Britain that people began to realize that the Nazis weren't the best customers in the world, but by then it was too late."

"It's like a mirror image of the world—a warped mirror," Dan said, drawing savagely on his cigarette. "While we were going around the moon something happened to change the whole world in the way it would have been if history had been altered some time in the early thirties."

"World didn't change, boys," Reeves said, "it's always been just the way it is now. Though I admit the way you tell it it sounds a lot better. But it's either the whole world or you, and I'm banking on the simpler of the two. Don't know what kind of an experiment the air corps had you two involved in but it must have addled your gray matter."

"I can't buy that," Gino insisted. "I know I'm beginning to feel like I have lost my marbles, but whenever I do I think about the capsule we landed in. How are you going to explain that away?"

"I'm not going to try. I know there are a lot of gadgets and things that got the engineers and the university profs tearing their hair out, but that doesn't bother me. I'm going back to the shooting war, where things are simpler. Until it is proved differently I think that you are both nuts, if you'll pardon the expression, sirs."

The official reaction in Denver was basically the same. A staff car, complete with MP outriders, picked them up as soon as they had landed at Lowry Field and took them directly to Fitzsimmons Hospital. They were taken directly to the laboratories, and what must have been a good half of a giant hospital's staff took turns prodding, questioning, and testing them. They were encouraged to speak—many times with lie-detector instrumentation attached to them—but none of their questions were answered. Occasional high-ranking officers looked on gloomily, but took no part in the examination. They talked for hours into tape recorders, answering questions in every possible field, from history to physics, and when they tired were kept going on benzedrine. There was more than a week of this in which they saw each other only by chance in the examining rooms, until they were weak from fatigue and hazy from the drugs. None of their questions were answered, they were just reassured that everything would be taken care of as soon as the examinations were over. When the interruption came it was a welcome surprise, and apparently unexpected. Gino was being probed by a drafted history professor who wore oxidized captain's bars and a gravy-stained battlejacket. Since his voice was hoarse from the days of prolonged questioning, Gino held the microphone close to his mouth and talked in a whisper.

"Can you tell me who was the Secretary of the Treasury under Lincoln?" the captain asked.

"How the devil should I know? And I doubt very much if there is anyone else in this hospital who knows—besides you. And do you know?"

"Of course—"

The door burst open and a full colonel with an MP brassard looked in. A very high-ranking messenger boy: Gino was impressed.

"I've come for Major Lombardi."

"You'll have to wait," the history captain protested, twisting his already rumpled necktie. "I've not finished . . ."

"That is not important. The major is to come with me at once."

They marched silently through a number of halls until they came to a dayroom where Dan was sprawled deep in a chair smoking a cigar. A loudspeaker on the wall was muttering in a monotone.

"Have a cigar," Dan called out, and pushed the package across the table.

"What's the drill now?" Gino asked, biting off the end and looking for a match.

"Another conference, big brass, lots of turmoil. We'll go in in a moment as soon as some of the shouting dies down. There is a theory now as to what happened, but not much agreement on it even though Einstein himself dreamed it up . . ."

"Einstein! But he's dead . . ."

"Not now he isn't, I've seen him. A grand old gent of over ninety, as fragile as a stick but still going strong. He . . . say wait—isn't that a news broadcast?"

They listened to the speaker that one of the MP's had turned up.

". . . in spite of fierce fighting the city of San Antonio is now in enemy hands. Up to an hour ago there were still reports from the surrounded Alamo where units of the Fifth Cavalry have refused to surrender, and all America has been following this second battle of the Alamo. History has repeated itself, tragically, because there now appears to be no hope that any survivors . . ."

"Will you gentlemen please follow me," a staff officer broke in, and the two astronauts went out after him. He knocked at a door and opened it for them. "If you please."

"I am very happy to meet you both," Albert Einstein said, and waved them to chairs.

He sat with his back to the window, his thin, white hair catching the afternoon sunlight and making an aura about his head.

"Professor Einstein," Dan Coye said, "can you tell us

what has happened? What has changed?"

"Nothing has changed; that is the important thing that you must realize. The world is the same and you are the same, but you have—for want of a better word I must say—*moved*. I am not being clear. It is easier to express in mathematics."

"Anyone who climbs into a rocket has to be a bit of a science-fiction reader, and I've absorbed my quota," Dan said. "Have we got into one of those parellel worlds things they used to write about, branches of time and all that?"

"No, what you have done is *not* like that, though it may be a help to you to think of it that way. This is the same *objective* world that you left—but not the same *subjective* one. There is only one galaxy that we inhabit, only one universe. But our awareness of it changes many of its aspects of reality."

"You've lost me," Gino sighed.

"Let me see if I get it," Dan said. "It sounds like you are saying that things are just as we think we see them, and our thinking keeps them that way. Like that tree in the quad I remember from college."

"Again not correct, but an approximation you may hold if it helps you to clarify your thinking. It is a phenomenon that I have long suspected, certain observations in the speed of light that might be instrumentation errors, gravitic phenomena, chemical reactions. I have suspected something, but have not known where to look. I thank you gentlemen from the bottom of my heart for giving me this opportunity at the very end of my life, for giving me the clues that may lead to a solution to this problem."

"Solution . . ." Gino's mouth opened. "Do you mean there is a chance we can go back to the world as we knew it?"

"Not only a chance—but the strongest possibility. What happened to you was an accident. You were away from the planet of your birth, away from its atmospheric envelope and, during parts of your orbit, even out of sight of it. Your sense of reality was badly strained, and your physical reality and the reality of your mental relationships were changed by the death of your comrade. All these combined to allow you to return to a world with a slightly different aspect of reality from the one you have left. The historians have pinpointed the point of change. It occurred on the seventeenth of August, 1933, the day that President Roosevelt died of pneumonia."

"Is that why all those medical questions about my childhood?" Dan asked. "I had pneumonia then, I was just a couple of months old, almost died; my mother told me about it often enough afterwards. It could have been at the same time. It isn't possible that I lived and the President died . . . ?"

Einstein shook his head. "No, you must remember that you both lived in the world as you knew it. The dynamics of the relationship are far from clear, though I do not doubt that there is some relationship involved. But that is not important. What is important is that I think I have developed a way to mechanically bring about the translation from one reality aspect to another. It will take years to develop it to translate matter from one reality to a different order, but it is perfected enough now—I am sure—to return matter that has already been removed from another order."

Gino's chair scraped back as he jumped to his feet. "Professor—am I right in saying, and I may have got you wrong, that you can take us and pop us back to where we came from?"

Einstein smiled. "Putting it as simply as you have, Major . . . the answer is *yes*. Arrangements are being made now to return both of you and your capsule as soon as possible. In return for which we ask you a favor."

"Anything, of course," Dan said, leaning forward.

"You will have the reality-translator machine with you, and microcopies of all our notes, theories, and practical conclusions. In the world that you come from, all of the massive forces of technology and engineering can be summoned to solve the problem of mechanically accomplishing what you both did once by accident. You might be able to do this within months, and that is all the time that there is left."

"Exactly what do you mean?"

"We are losing the war. In spite of all the warning, we were not prepared; we thought it would never come to us.

The Nazis advance on all fronts. It is only a matter of time until they win. We can still win, but only with your atom bombs."

"You don't have atomic bombs now?" Gino asked.

Einstein sat silent for a moment before he answered. "No, there was no opportunity. I have always been sure that they could be constructed, but have never put it to the test. The Germans felt the same, and at one time even had a heavy water project that aimed toward controlled nuclear fission. But their military successes were so great that they abandoned it along with other far-fetched and expensive schemes, such as the hollow-globe theory. I myself have never wanted to see this hellish thing built, and from what you have told me about it, it is worse than my most terrible dream. But I approached the President about it, when the Nazi threat was closing in, but nothing was done. Too expensive. Now it is too late. But perhaps it isn't. If *your* America will help us, the enemy will be defeated. And after that, what a wealth of knowledge we shall have once our worlds are in contact. Will you do it?"

"Of course," Dan Coye said. "But the brass will take a lot of convincing. I suggest some films be made of you and others explaining some of this. And enclose some documents, anything that will help convince them of what has happened."

"I can do something better," Einstein said, taking a small bottle from a drawer of the table. "Here is a recently developed drug, and the formula, that has proved effective in arresting certain of the more violent forms of cancer. This is an example of what I mean by the profit that can accrue when our two worlds can exchange information."

Dan pocketed the precious bottle as they turned to leave. With a sense of awe they gently shook hands with the frail old man who had been dead many years in the world they knew, to which they would be soon returning.

The military moved fast. A large jet bomber was quickly converted to carry one of the American solid-fuel rocket missiles. Not yet operational, it was doubtful if they ever would be at the rate of the Nazi advance. But given an aerial boost by the bomber it could reach up out of the ionosphere—carrying the payload of the moon capsule with its two pilots. Clearing the fringes of the atmosphere was essential to the operation of the instrument that was to return them to what they could only think of as their own world. It seemed preposterously tiny to be able to change worlds.

"Is that *all?*" Gino asked when they settled themselves back into the capsule. A square case, containing records and reels of film, was strapped between their seats. On top of it rested a small gray metal box.

"What do you expect—an atom smasher?" Dan asked, checking out the circuits. The capsule had been restored as much as was possible to the condition it was in the day it had landed. The men wore their pressure suits. "We came here originally by accident, by just thinking wrong or something like that, if my theory's correct."

"It isn't—but neither is mine, so we can't let it bug us."

"Yeah, I see what you mean. The whole crazy business may not be simple, but the mechanism doesn't have to be physically complex. All we have to do is throw the switch, right?"

"Roger. The thing is self-powered. We'll be tracked by radar, and when we hit apogee in our orbit they'll give us a signal on our usual operating frequency. We throw the switch—and drop."

"Drop right back to where we came from, I hope."

"Hello there, cargo," a voice crackled over the speaker. "Pilot here. We are about to take off. All set?"

"In the green, all circuits," Dan reported, and settled back.

The big bomber rumbled the length of the field and slowly pulled itself into the air, heavily, under the weight of the rocket slung beneath its belly. The capsule was in the nose of the rocket and all the astronauts could see was the shining skin of the mother ship. It was a rough ride. The mathematics had indicated that probability of success would be greater over Florida and the south Atlantic, the original reentry target. This meant penetrating enemy territory. The passengers could not see the battle being fought by the accompanying jet fighters, and the pilot of the converted bomber did not tell them. It was a fierce battle and at one point almost a lost one: only a suicidal crash by one of the escort fighters prevented an enemy jet from attacking the mother ship.

"Stand by for drop," the radio said, and a moment later came the familiar sensation of free fall as the rocket dropped clear of the plane. Preset controls timed the ignition and orbit. Acceleration pressed them into their couches.

A sudden return to weightlessness was acompanied by the tiny explosions as the carrying-rocket blasted free the explosive bolts that held it to the capsule. For a measureless time their inertia carried them higher in their orbit while gravity tugged back. The radio crackled with a carrier wave, then a voice broke in.

"Be ready with the switch . . . ready to throw it . . . NOW!"

Dan flipped the switch and nothing happened. Nothing that they could perceive in any case. They looked at each other silently, then at the altimeter as they dropped back toward the distant Earth.

"Get ready to open the chute," Dan said heavily, just as a roar of sound burst from the radio.

"Hello Apollo, is that you? This is Kennedy control, can you hear me? Repeat—can you hear me? Can you answer . . . in heaven's name, Dan, are you there . . . are you there . . . ?"

The voice was almost hysterical, bubbling over itself. Dan flipped the talk button.

"Dan Coye here—is that you, Skipper?"

"Yes—but how did you get there? Where have you been since . . . cancel, repeat cancel that last. We have you on the screen and you will hit in the sea and we have ships standing by . . ."

The two astronauts met each other's eyes and smiled. Gino raised his thumb up in a token of victory. They had done it. Behind the controlled voice that issued them instructions they could feel the riot that must be breaking after their unexpected arrival. To the observers on Earth —*this* Earth—they must have vanished on the other side of the moon. Then reappeared suddenly some weeks later, alive and sound, long days after their oxygen and supplies should have been exhausted. There would be a lot to explain.

It was a perfect landing. The sun shone, the sea was smooth, there was scarcely any cross wind. They resurfaced within seconds and had a clear view through their port over the small waves. A cruiser was already headed their way, only a few miles off.

"It's over," Dan said with an immense sigh of relief as he unbuckled himself from the chair.

"Over!" Gino said in a choking voice. "Over? Look—look at the flag there!"

The cruiser turned tightly, the flag on its stern standing out proudly in the air. The red and white stripes of Old Glory, the fifty white stars on the field of deepest blue.

And in the middle of the stars, in the center of the blue rectangle, lay a golden crown.

COMMANDO RAID

Private Truscoe and the captain had left the truck, parked out of sight in the jungle, and had walked a good hundred yards further down the road. They were crouched now in the dense shadows of the trees, with the silver light of the full moon picking out every rut and hollow of the dirt track before them.

"Be quiet!" the captain whispered, putting a restraining hand on the soldier's arm, listening. Truscoe held his breath and struggled to keep absolutely still. Captain Carter was a legendary jungle fighter, with the scars and medals to prove it. If he thought there was something dangerous, creeping closer in the darkness . . . Truscoe suppressed an involuntary shudder.

"It's all right," the captain said, this time in a normal speaking tone. "Something big out there, buffalo or deer. But it's downwind and it took off as soon as it caught our smell. You can smoke if you want to."

The soldier hesitated, not sure how to answer. Finally, he said, "Sir, aren't we supposed . . . I mean someone could see the flame?"

"We're not hiding, Private Truscoe. William—do they call you Billy?"

"Why, yes sir."

"We picked this spot, Billy, because none of the locals normally come this way at night. Light up. The smoke will let all the wildlife know that we're here and they'll keep their distance. They are a lot more afraid of us than you are of them. And our informant can find us by the smell too. One whiff and he'll know that it's not the local leaf. That trail over there leads to the village and he'll probably come that way."

Billy looked but could see neither trail nor opening in the jungle wall where the officer pointed. But if the captain said so it had to be true. He clutched his M-16 rifle tightly and looked around at the buzzing, clattering darkness.

"It's not so much the critters out there, sir. I've done plenty of hunting in Alabama and I know this gun can stop anything around. Except maybe another gun. I mean, this geek, sir, the one that's coming. Isn't he kind of a traitor? You know, if he finks on his own people how do we know he won't do the same to us?"

Carter's voice was patient and gave no indication of how much he loathed the word *geek*.

"The man's an informant, not a traitor, and he is more eager than we are for this deal to go through. He was originally a refugee from a village in the south, one that was wiped out by that earthquake some years back. You have to understand that these people are very provincial, and he'll be a 'foreigner' in this village as long as he lives. His wife is dead, he has nothing to stay here for. When we approached him for information he jumped at the chance. We'll pay him enough so that he won't ever have to work again. He'll retire to a village close to the one where he was raised. It's a good deal."

Billy was emboldened by the darkness and the presence of the solitary officer. "Still, seems sort of raw for the people he lived with. Selling them out."

"No one is being sold out." The captain was much more positive now. "What we are doing for them is for their own good. They may not see it that way now, but it is. It is the long-term results that count."

The captain sounded a little peeved. Billy shifted uneasily and did not answer. He should have remembered you don't talk to officers like they were real people or something.

"Stand up, here he comes," Carter said.

Billy had the feeling that maybe the captain could have outhunted him even in his own stand of woods back in Alabama. He neither saw nor heard a thing. Only when the short, turbaned figure appeared at their sides did he know that the informant had arrived.

"*Tuan?*" the man whispered, and Carter spoke to him

quietly in his own tongue. It was so much geek talk to Billy: they had had lectures on the language, but he had never bothered to listen. When they stepped out into the flood of moonlight he saw that the man was a typical geek, too. Scrawny and little and old. There was more cloth in the turban than in his loincloth. All of his possessions, the accumulation of a lifetime, were rolled in a straw mat that he carried in one hand. And he sounded frightened.

"Let's get back to the truck," Captain Carter ordered. "He won't talk here. Too afraid the villagers will find him."

He'd got cause to worry, Billy thought, following the disproportionate pair back down the road. The captain was half bent over as he talked to the little man.

Once the truck had coughed to life and the driver was tooling her back to camp the informant relaxed. He talked steadily in a high, birdlike voice, and the captain put a sheet of paper on his map case and sketched in the details of the village and the surrounding area. Billy nodded, bored, with his rifle between his legs, looking forward to some chow and hitting the sack. There was an all-night cook in the MP mess who would fry up steak and eggs for you if you were on night duty. The voice twittered on and the map grew.

"Don't want to drop government property, do you, Billy?" Carter asked, and Billy realized that he had dozed off and the M-16 had fallen from his fingers. But the captain had caught it and held it safe for him. The sharp blue illumination of the mercury vapor lights of the camp poured into the open back of the truck. Billy opened his mouth, but did not know what to say. Then the officer was gone, with the tiny native scrambling after him, and Billy was alone. He jumped down, boots squelching in the mud, and stretched. Even though the captain had saved his neck rather than report him, he still wasn't sure whether he liked him or not.

Less than three hours after he had fallen asleep the light came on above him in the tent, and the recorded notes of reveille sawed out of the speaker mounted next to it. Billy blinked at his watch and saw that it was just after two.

"What the hell is all this about?" someone shouted. "Another damn night maneuver?"

Billy knew, but before he could open his mouth the CO came on the speaker and told them first.

"We're going in, men. This is it. The first units jump off in two hours' time. H Hour will be at first light, at exactly 0515. Your unit commanders will give you complete and detailed instructions before we roll. Full field packs. This is what you have been training for—and this is the moment that you have been waiting for. Don't get rattled, do your job, and don't believe all the latrine rumors that you hear. I'm talking particularly to you new men. I know you have been chewed out a lot, and you have been called 'combat virgins' and a lot worse. Forget it. You're a team now—and after tomorrow you won't even be virgins."

The men laughed at that, but not Billy. He recognized the old bushwa when it was being fed to him. At home, at school, it was the same old crap. Do or die for our dear old High. Crap.

"Let's go, let's go," the sergeant shouted, throwing open the flap of the tent. "We don't have all night and you guys are creeping around like grandmas in a sack race."

That was more like it. The sergeant didn't horse around. With him you knew just where you stood, all the time.

"Roll the packs tighter, they look like they're stuffed full of turds." The sergeant had never really taken the orders on use of language to heart.

It was still hot, dark and hot and muggy, and Billy could feel the sweat already soaking into his clean dungarees. They double-timed to chow, stuffed it down, and double-timed back. Then, packs on backs, they lined up at the QM stores for field issue. A tired and yellowish corporal signed in Billy's M-16, checked the serial number, then handed him a Mark-13 and a sack of reloads. The cool metal slipped through Billy's hands and he almost dropped it.

"Keep that flitgun out of the mud or you'll be signing a statement of charges for life." The corporal growled, by reflex, and was already turning to the next man.

Billy gave him the finger—as soon as his back was

turned—and went out into the company street. Under a light he looked at the riot gun, turning it over and over. It was new, right out of the Cosmoline, smooth and shining, with a wide stock, a thick barrel, and a thicker receiver. Heavy, too, eighteen pounds, but he didn't mind.

"Fall in, fall in," the sergeant was still in good voice.

They fell into ranks and waited at ease for a long time. Hurry up and wait, it was always like this, and Billy slipped a piece of gum into his mouth when all the noncoms had their backs turned, then chewed it slowly. His squad was finally called out and dogtrotted off to the copters, where Captain Carter was waiting.

"Just one thing before we board," the captain said. "You men here are in the shock squad and you have the dirty work to do. I want you to stay behind me at all times, in loose order, and watch on all sides and still watch me at the same time. We can expect trouble. But no matter what happens, do not—and I repeat that—do *not* act upon your own initiative. Look to me for orders. We want this to be a model operation and we don't want any losses."

He unrolled a big, diagrammatic map, then pointed to the front rank. "You two men, hold this up so the others can see. This is the target we are going to hit. The village is on the river, with the rice fields between it and the houses. The hovercraft will come in right over the fields, so no one will get out that way. There is a single dirt road in through the jungle, and that will be plugged, and there will be squads on every trail out of there. The villagers can dive into the jungle if they want, but they won't get far. They'll have to cut their way through and we can follow them easily and bring them back. There are men assigned to all these duties and they will all be in position at H Hour. Then we hit. We come in low and fast so we can sit down in the center of the houses, in this open spot, before anyone even knows that we are on the way. If we do it right the only resistance will be the dogs and chickens."

"Shoot the dogs and eat the chickens," someone shouted from the back, and everyone laughed. The captain smiled slightly to show that he appreciated the joke, but disapproved of chatter while they were fallen in. He tapped the map.

"As we touch down the other units will move in. The headman in the village, this is his house here, is an old rogue with military service and a bad temper. Everyone will be too shocked to provide much resistance—unless he orders it. I'll take care of him. Now—are there any questions?" He looked around at the silent men. "All right then, let's load up."

The big, double-rotored copters squatted low, their wide doors close to the ground. As soon as the men were aboard, the starters whined and the long blades began to turn slowly. The operation had begun.

When they rose above the trees they could see the lightening of the eastern horizon. They stayed low, their wheels almost brushing the leaves, like a flock of ungainly birds of prey. It wasn't a long flight, but the sudden tropical dawn was on them almost before they realized it.

The ready light flashed on and the captain came down from the cockpit and gave them the thumbs-up signal. They went in.

It was a hard landing, almost a drop, and the doors banged open as they touched. The shock squad hit the ground and Captain Carter went first.

The pounded dirt compound was empty. The squad formed on the captain and watched the doorways of the rattan-walled buildings, where people were beginning to appear. The surprise had been absolute. There was the grumble of truck engines from the direction of the road and a roar of sound from the river. Billy glanced that way and saw the hovercraft moving over the paddies in a cloud of spray. Then he jumped, raising the riot gun, as a shrill warbling ripped at his ears.

It was the captain. He had a voice gun with a built-in siren. The sound wailed, shriller and shriller, then died away as he flipped the switch. He raised it and spoke into the microphone, and his voice filled the village.

Billy couldn't understand the geek talk, but it sounded impressive. For the first time he realized that the captain was unarmed—and even wore a garrison cap instead of his helmet. That was taking a big chance. Billy raised the flitgun to the ready and glanced around at the people who were slowly emerging from the houses.

Then the captain pointed toward the road and his echoing voice stopped. All of the watching heads, as though worked by a single string, turned to look where he indicated. A half-track appeared, engine bellowing, trailing a thick column of dust. It braked, skidding to a stop, and a corporal jumped from the back and ran the few paces to the town well. He had a bulky object in his arms, which he dropped into the well—then dived aside.

With a sharp explosion the well blew up. Dirt flew and mud and water spattered down. The walls collapsed. Where the well had once been there remained only a shallow, smoking pit. The captain's voice cut through the shocked silence that followed.

Yet, even as his first amplified words swept the compound, a hoarse shout interrupted them. A gray-haired man had emerged from the headman's house. He was shouting, pointing at the captain, who waited, then answered back. He was interrupted before he was finished. The captain tried to argue, but the headman ran back inside the building.

He was fast. A moment later he came out—with an archaic steel helmet on his head, waving a long-bladed sword over his head. There hadn't been a helmet made like that in forty years. And a *sword*. Billy almost laughed out loud until he realized that the headman was playing it for real. He ran at the captain, sword raised, ignoring the captain's voice completely. It was like watching a play, being in a play, with no one moving and only the captain and the old man playing their roles.

The headman wasn't listening. He attacked, screeching, and brought the sword down and around in a wicked, decapitating cut. The captain blocked the blow with the voice gun, which coughed and died. He was still trying to reason with the old man, but his voice sounded smaller and different now—and the headman wasn't listening.

Twice he struck, and a third time, and each time the captain backed away a bit and parried with the voice gun, which was rapidly being reduced to battered junk. As the sword came up again, the captain called back over his shoulder.

"Private Truscoe, take this man out. This has gone far enough."

Billy was well trained and knew what to do without

even thinking about it. A step forward, the flitgun raised to his shoulder and aimed, the safety off, and when the old man's head filled the sight he squeezed off the shot.

With a throat-clearing cough the cloud of compressed gas blasted out and struck the headman full in the face.

"Masks on," Captain Carter ordered, and once more the movement was automatic.

Small of the stock in his left hand, right hand free, grasp the handle (gas mask, actuating) under the brim of his helmet, and pull. The transparent plastic reeled down and he hooked it under his chin. All by the numbers.

But then something went wrong. The Mace-IV that the flitgun expelled was supposed to take anyone out. Down and out. But the headman was not going down. He was retching, his belly working in and out uncontrollably, while the vomit ran down his chin and onto his bare chest. He still clutched the long sword and, with his free hand, he threw his helmet to the ground and pried open one streaming eye. He must have made out Billy's form through his tears, because he turned from the captain and came on, sword raised, staggering.

Billy brought the flitgun up, but it was in his left hand and he couldn't fire. He changed the grip, fumbling with it, but the man was still coming on. The sword glistened as the rising sun struck it.

Billy swung the gun around like a club and caught the headman across the temple with the thick barrel. The man pitched face forward to the ground and was still.

Billy pointed the gun down at him and pulled the trigger, again and again, the gas streaming out and covering the sprawled figure . . .

Until the captain knocked the gun from his hand and pulled him about, almost throwing him to the ground.

"Medic!" The captain shouted then, almost whispering through his clenched teeth, "You fool, you fool."

Billy just stood, dazed, trying to understand what had happened, as the ambulance pulled up. There were injections, cream on the man's face, oxygen from a tank, then he was loaded onto a stretcher and the doctor came over.

"It's touch and go, captain. Possible skull fracture, and he breathed in a lot of your junk. How did it happen?"

"It will be in my report," Captain Carter answered in a toneless voice.

The doctor started to speak, thought better of it, and turned and climbed into the ambulance. It pulled away, dodging around the big trucks that were coming into the village. The people were out of the houses now, huddled in knots, talking under their breaths. There would be no more resistance.

Billy was aware that the captain was looking at him, looking as if he wanted to kill. The gas mask was suddenly hot on Billy's face and he pulled it free.

"It wasn't my fault, sir," Billy explained. "He just came at me . . ."

"He came at me too. I didn't fracture his skull. It *was* your fault."

"No, it's not. Not when some old geek swings a rusty damn pig-sticker at me."

"He is not a geek, Private, but a citizen of this country and a man of stature in this village. He was defending his home and was within his rights—"

Billy was angry now. He knew it was all up with him and the Corps and his plans, and he didn't give a damn. He turned to the officer, fists clenched.

"He's a crummy geek from geeksville, and if he got rights what are we doing here, just tell me that?"

The captain was coldly quiet now. "We were invited here by the country's President and the Parliament, you know that as well as I do." His voice was drowned out as a truck passed close by and the exhaust blatted out at them. It stopped and men jumped down and began to unload lengths of plastic piping. Billy looked the captain square in the eye and told him off, what he had always wanted to say.

"In a pig's ass we were invited here. Some bigshot these local geeks never heard of says okay and we drop down their throats and spend a couple billion dollars of the US taxpayers' money to give some geeks the good life they don't know nothing about and don't need—so what the hell!" He shouted the last words. The captain was much quieter.

"I suppose it would be better if we helped them the way

we helped in Vietnam? Came in and burned them and shot them and blasted them right back to the Stone Age?"

Another truck stopped and began unloading sinks, toilets, electric stoves.

"Well, why not? Why not! If they trouble Uncle Sam— then knock them out. We don't need anything from these kind of broken-down raggedy people. Now Uncle Sam is Uncle Sap and taking care of the world and the taxpayers are footing the bill . . ."

"Shut up and listen, Private." There was an edge to the captain's voice that Billy had never heard before and he shut up. "I don't know how you got into the Aid Corps, but I do know that you don't belong in it. This is one world and it gets smaller every year. The Eskimos in the Arctic have DDT poisoning from the farms in the Midwest. The strontium ninety from a French atom test in the Pacific gives bone cancer to a child in New York. This is spaceship Earth and we're all aboard it together, trying to stay alive on it. The richest countries better help the poorest ones because it's all the same spaceship. And it's already almost too late. In Vietnam we spent five million dollars a head to kill the citizens of that country, and our profit was the undying hatred of everyone there, both north and south, and the loathing of the civilized world. We've made our mistakes, now let's profit from them.

"For far less than one thousandth of the cost of killing a man, and making his friends our enemies, we can save a life and make the man our friend. Two hundred bucks a head, that's what this operation costs. We've blown up the well here because it was a cesspit of infection, and we are drilling a new well to bring up pure water from the strata below. We are putting toilets into the houses, and sinks. We are killing the disease-breeding insects. We are running in power lines and bringing in a medical mission to save their lives. We are opening a birth-control clinic so they can have families like people, not breed like rats and pull the world down with them. They are going to have scientific agriculture so they can eat better, and education so they can be more than working animals. We are going to bring them about five percent of the 'benefits' you enjoy in the sovereign state of Alabama and we are doing it from selfish motives. We want to stay alive. But at least we are doing it."

The captain looked at his clenched fist, then slowly opened it. "Sergeant," he called out as he turned away. "Put this man under arrest and see that he is sent back to the camp at once."

A crate of flush toilets thudded to the ground almost at Billy's feet and a thread of hot anger snapped inside of him. Who were these people to get waited on like this? He had grown up in a sharecropper's shack and had never seen a toilet like these until he was more than eight years old. Now he had to help give them away to . . .

"Niggers, that's what these people are! And we give them everything on a silver platter. It's bleeding hearts like you, Captain, crying your eyes out for these poor helpless people, that are causing the trouble!"

Captain Carter stopped, and slowly turned about. He looked at the young man who stood before him and felt only a terrible feeling of depression.

"No, Private William Truscoe, I don't cry for these people. I don't cry. But if I ever could I would cry for you."

After that he went away.

NOT ME, NOT AMOS CABOT!

The morning mail had arrived while Amos Cabot was out shopping and had been thrown onto the rickety table in the front hall. He poked through it even though he knew there would be nothing for him; this wasn't the right day. On the thirteenth his Social Security check came and on the twenty-fourth the union check, there never was anything else except for a diminishing number of cards every Christmas. Nothing, he knew it. A large blue envelope was propped against the mirror but he couldn't make out the name, damn that skinflint Mrs. Peavey and her two-watt bulbs. He bent over and blinked at it—then blinked again. By God it was for him, and no mistake! Felt like a thick magazine or a catalog: he wondered what it could possibly be and who might have sent it to him. Clutching it to his chest with a knobby and liver-spotted hand he began the long drag up the three flights of stairs to his room. He dropped his string bag with the two cans of beans and the loaf of day-old white bread onto the drainboard and sat down heavily in his chair by the window. Unsealing the envelope he saw that it was a magazine, a thick glossy one with a black cover. He slid it out onto his lap and stared at it with horrified eyes.

Hereafter the title read in black, prickly gothic letters against a field of greenish-gray, and underneath it was subtitled *The Magazine of Preparedness*. The rest of the cover was black, solid midnight black, except for an inset photograph shaped like a tombstone that had a cheerful view of a cemetery filled with flower blossoms, ranked headstones, and brooding mausoleums. Was this all a very bad joke? It didn't seem so as Amos flipped through the

110

pages, catching quick glimpses of caskets, coffins, cemetery plots, and urns of mortal ashes. With a grunt of disgust he threw the magazine onto the table and as he did so a letter fell out and drifted to the floor. It was addressed to him, on the magazine's stationery, there was no mistake.

My Dearest Sir:

Welcome to the contented family of happy readers of Hereafter—The Magazine of Preparedness *that smooths the road ahead. You, who are about to die, we salute you! A long, happy life lies behind you and ahead the Gates of Eternity are swinging open to welcome you, to return you to the bosom of your loved ones long since passed on. Now, at this friendly final hour, we stand behind you ready to help you on your way. Have you settled your will? Bet you've been remiss—but that's no problem now! Just turn to page 109 and read the inspirational article "Where There's a Will" and learn all there is to know. And then, on page 114, you'll find a full-sized, fold-out will that can be torn out along the handy perforations. Just fill in the few blanks, sign your name and have your local notary public (he's usually in the stationery store!) witness the signature. Don't delay! And have you considered cremation? There is a wonderfully inspirational message from Dr. Phillip Musgrove of The Little Church Around the Corner from the Crematorium on page. . . .*

Amos picked up the magazine with shaking hands and threw it the length of the room, feeling slightly better when it tore in two.

"What do you mean I'm going to die—what do you say that for?" he shouted, then lowered his voice as Antonelli next door hammered on the wall. "What's the idea of sending a filthy thing like that to a person? What's the idea?"

What was the idea? He picked the two halves of the magazine up and smoothed them out on the table. It was all too good-looking, too expensive to be a joke—these were real ads. After some searching he found the contents page and worked his way through the fine print, which he could hardly read, until he came to the publisher's name: Saxon-Morris Publishers, Inc. and they must have money because they were in the Saxon-Morris Building, he knew it, one of the new granite slabs on Park Avenue.

They weren't getting away with it! A spark of anger blazed bravely in Amos Cabot's thin bosom. He had made the Fifth Avenue Coach Company send him a letter of apology about the way that driver had talked to him on St. Patrick's day, and the Triborough Automatic Drink Company had refunded him fifty cents in stamps for coins their machines had consumed without giving refreshment in return. Now Saxon-Morris was going to find out that they couldn't get away with it either!

It had been warm out, but March was a changeable month so he put on his heavy wool muffler. A couple of dollars should more than cover the costs of the excursion, bus fares, and a cup of tea in the Automat, so he took two wrinkled bills from behind the sugar can. Watch out, Saxon-Morris, you just watch out.

It was very difficult to see anyone at Saxon-Morris without an appointment. The girl with upswept red hair and layers of glazed makeup wasn't even sure that they had a magazine called *Hereafter*. There was a list of all the Saxon-Morris publications on the wall behind her red, kidney-shaped desk, but the gold letters on dark green marble were hard to read in the dim light. When he kept insisting she searched through a booklet of names and telephone numbers and finally, reluctantly, agreed that it was one of their magazines.

"I want to see the editor."

"Which editor is it you want to see?"

"Any editor, don't matter a damn." Her cold manner became even colder when the word touched her.

"Might I ask your business?"

"That's my business. Let me see the editor."

It was more than an hour before she found someone whom he could see, or perhaps she just grew tired of his sitting there and glowering at her. After a number of muffled conversations she hung up the phone.

"If you just go through that door there first turn to the right then up one half flight, fourth door on the left, Mr. Mercer will see you Room seven eighty-two."

Amos was instantly lost in the maze of passages and gray doors, but the second time he stumbled into a mail room one of the bored youths led him to 782. He pushed in without knocking.

"You Mercer, the editor of *Hereafter?*"

"Yes, I'm Mercer." He was a chubby man with a round face and rounder glasses, squeezed behind a desk that filled the end of the tiny and windowless office. "But this is circulation, not editorial. The girl at the front desk said you had a circulation problem."

"I got a problem all right—why you sending me your blasted magazine that I don't want?"

"Well—perhaps I can help you there, which publication are you referring to . . . ?"

"*Hereafter,* that's the one."

"Yes, that's one in my group." Mercer opened two files before he found the right folder, then he scratched through it and came up with a sheet of paper. "I'm afraid I can't be of any help to you, Mr. Cabot, you must be on the free-subscription list and we can't cancel them. Sorry."

"What do you mean, *sorry!* I don't want the filthy thing and you better stop sending it!"

Mercer tried to be friendly and succeeded in conjuring up an artificial smile. "Let's be reasonable, Mr. Cabot, that's a high-quality magazine and you are receiving it for nothing; why a subscription costs ten dollars a year! If you have been lucky enough to be chosen for a free sub you shouldn't complain . . ."

"Who chose me for a free subscription, I didn't send anything in."

"No, you wouldn't have to. Your name probably appeared on one of the lists that we purchase from insurance companies, veterans hospitals, and the like. *Hereafter* is one of our throwaway magazines; of course I don't mean that we throw them away, on the contrary they go to very selected subscribers, and we don't make our costs back from subscriptions but from the advertisers' fees. In a sense they underwrite the costs of these fine magazines, so you can say it is sort of a public service. For new mothers, for instance, we buy lists from all the hospitals and send out six-month subs of *Your Baby,* with some really fine advice and articles, and of course the ads, which are educational in themselves . . ."

"Well, I'm no new mother! Why you sending me your rag?"

"Hereafter is a bit different from *Your Baby*, but is still a service publication. It's a matter of statistics, sir. Every day just so many people die, of certain ages and backgrounds and that kind of thing. The people in the insurance companies, actuaries I think they call them, keep track of all these facts and figures and draw up plenty of graphs and tables. Very accurate, they assure me. They have life expectancy down to a fine art. They take a man, say, like yourself, of a certain age, background, physical fitness, environment, and so on, and pinpoint the date of death very exactly. Not the day and hour and that kind of thing—I suppose they could if they wanted to—but for our purposes a period of two years is satisfactory. This gives us a number of months and issues to acquaint the subscriber with our magazine and the services offered by our advertisers, so by the time the subscriber dies the ad messages will have reached saturation."

"Are you telling me I'm going to die inside the next two years?" Amos shrieked hoarsely, flushing with anger.

"I'm not telling you, sir, no indeed!" Mercer drew away a bit and wiped some of the old man's spittle from his glasses with his handkerchief. "That is the actuaries' job. Their computer has come up with your name and sent it to me. They say you will die within two years. As a public service we send you *Hereafter*. A service—nothing more."

"I ain't going to die in two years, not me! Not Amos Cabot!"

"That is entirely up to you, sir. My position here is just a routine one. Your subscription has been entered and will be canceled only when a copy is returned with the imprint *addressee deceased*."

"I'm not going to die!"

"That might possibly happen, though I can't recall any cases offhand. But since it is a two-year subscription I imagine it will expire automatically at the end of the second year, if not canceled beforehand. Yes, that's what would happen."

It ruined Amos's day, and though the sun was shining warmly he never noticed it. He went home and thought so much about the whole thing that he couldn't sleep. The next day was no better and he began to wonder if this was part of the message the dreadful magazine had conveyed. If death was close by—they were so sure of it—why did he not relax and agree with them? Send in his will, order the plot, tomb, gravestone, Last Message forms, and quietly expire.

"No! They'll not do it to me!"

At first he thought he would wait for next month's copy and write *addressee deceased* and send it back to them, that would stop the copies coming sure enough. Then he remembered fat little Mercer and could see his happy expression when the cancellation crossed his desk. Right again, dead on schedule as always. Old fool should have known you can't lick statistics. Old fool indeed! He would show them. The Cabots were a long-lived family no matter what the records said, and a hardheaded one too. They weren't going to kill him off that easily.

After much wheedling he got in to see the doctor at his old union and talked him into making a complete and thorough physical checkup.

"Not bad, not bad at all for an old boy," the doctor told him while he was buttoning his shirt.

"I'm only seventy-two; that's not old!"

"Of course it's not," the doctor said soothingly. "Just statistics, you know; a man of your age with your background . . ."

"I know all about those damned statistics; I didn't come to you for that. What's the report say?"

"You can't complain about your physical shape, Amos," he said, scanning the sheet. "Blood pressure looks all right, but you're leaning toward anemia. Do you eat much liver and fresh greens?"

"Hate liver. Greens cost too much."

"That's your choice. But remember—you can't take it with you. Spend some more money on food. Give your heart a break—don't climb too many stairs."

"I live three flights up; how do I avoid stairs?"

"That's your choice again. If you want to take care of the old ticker move to the ground floor. And vitamin D in the winter and . . ."

There was more, and after he had swallowed his first anger Amos made notes. There were food and vitamins and sleep and fresh air and a whole list of nonsense as long as your arm. But there was also the two-year subscription of *Hereafter,* so he bent back over his notes.

Without his realizing why, the next months passed quickly. He was busy, finding a room on the ground floor, changing his eating habits, getting settled in his new place. At first he used to throw out *Hereafter* whenever its gloomy bulk shadowed his mail slot, but when a year had passed he grew bolder. There was an ad for mausoleums and one of the finest had a big tag on it labeled in red *Reserved for You. Not for me!!!* he scrawled above and tore it from the magazine and mounted it on the wall. He followed it with other pictures, friendly gravediggers beckoning toward raw openings in the earth, cut-to-order coffins with comfortable padding, and all the rest. When eighteen months had passed he enjoyed himself throwing darts at "A Photograph of the Founder of Incino-Top-Rate, the Urn for Eternity," and carefully checked off the passing days on the calendar.

Only in the final few months did he begin to worry. He felt fine and the union doctor congratulated him for being a great example, but this didn't matter. Were the actuaries right—had his time almost run out? He could have worried himself to death, but that was not the way Cabots died! He would face this out and win.

First there were weeks left, then only days. The last five days before the copy was due he locked himself in his room and had the delicatessen send up food. It was expensive but he wasn't going to risk any accidents in the street, not now. He had received his twenty-four copies and his subscription should have expired. The next morning would tell. He could not fall asleep at all that night, even though he knew that regular sleep was important, but just lay there until the sky brightened. He dozed for a bit then, but woke up as soon as he heard the postman's footsteps outside. This was the day, would the magazine be there? His heart was pounding and he made himself go slow as he got into the bathrobe. His room was the first on the ground floor, right next to the entrance, and all he had to do was step out into the hall and open the front door.

"Morning," he said to the postman.

"Yeah," the man answered, slinging his heavy bag around and digging into it. Amos closed the door first—then feverishly went through the mail.

It wasn't there.

He had won!

If this was not the happiest day in his life it was close to it. Besides this his victories over the bus company and the coin machine crooks were nothing. This was a war won, not a battle. He'd licked them, licked their statistics and actuaries, accountants, mechanical brains, card files, clerks, and editors. He had won! He drank a beer—the first one in two years—then another, and laughed and talked with the gang at the bar. He had won. He fell into bed late and slept like a log until he was dragged awake by his landlady knocking on the door.

"Mail for you, Mr. Cabot. Mail."

Fear gripped him, then slowly ebbed away. It couldn't be. In two years *Hereafter* had never been late once, not one day. It must be some other mail—though this wasn't his check day. He slowly opened the door and took the large envelope, his grip so loose that it almost fell from his fingers.

Only when he had laid it on the bed did he breathe naturally again—it wasn't *Hereafter* in its vile blue envelope; this one was a gentle pink. It did contain a magazine though, just about the size of *Hereafter,* a bulky magazine with lots of pages. Its title was *Senility*—and the black letters were drawn in such a way that they looked as though they were made of cracked and crumbling stone—and underneath it said *The Magazine of Geri-ART-trics.* There was a picture of a feeble old man in a wheelchair with a blanket around his shoulders, sucking water through a curved glass tube. Inside was more. Ads for toilet chairs and hemorrhoid cushions, crutches and crank beds, articles on "Learn Braille When the Eyesight Goes," and "Happy Though Bedridden," and "Immobile for Twenty-five Years." A letter dropped out of the magazine and he half-read phrases here and there.

Welcome to the family . . . the magazine of geri-ART-trics that teaches you the art of growing old . . . many long years ahead of you . . . empty years . . . what happiness to

*find a copy in your mailbox every month . . . speaking
book edition for the blind . . . Braille for the blind and
deaf . . . every month . . .*

There were tears in his eyes when he looked up. It was
dark, a rainy and cold April morning with the wind rattling the window. Raindrops ran down the glass like great,
cold tears.

THE SECRET OF STONEHENGE

Low clouds rushed by overhead in the dusk and there was a spattering of sleet in the air. When Dr. Lanning opened the cab door of the truck the wind pounced on him, fresh from the Arctic, hurtling unimpeded across Salisbury Plain. He buried his chin in his collar and went around to the rear doors. Barker followed him out and tapped on the door of the little office nearby. There was no answer.

"Not so good," Lanning said, gently sliding the bulky wooden box down to the ground. "We don't leave our national monuments unguarded in the States."

"Really," Barker said, turning and striding to the gate in the wire fence. "Then I presume those initials carved in the base of the Washington Monument are neolithic graffiti. As you see I brought the key."

He unlocked the gate and threw it open with a squeal of unoiled hinges, then went to help Lanning with the case.

In the evening, under a lowering sky, that is the only way to see Stonehenge, without the ice cream cornets and clambering children. The Plain settles flat upon the earth, pressed outward to a distant horizon, and only the gray pillars of the sarsen stones have the strength to push up skyward.

Lanning led the way, bending into the wind, up the broad path of the Avenue. "They're always bigger than you expect them to be," he said, and Barker did not answer him, perhaps because it was true. They stopped next to the Altar Stone and lowered the case. "We'll know soon enough," Lanning said, throwing open the latches.

"Another theory?" Barker asked, interested in spite of himself. "Our megaliths seem to hold a certain fascination for you and your fellow Americans."

"We tackle our problems wherever we find them," Lanning answered, opening the cover and disclosing a chunky and complicated piece of apparatus mounted on an aluminum tripod. "I have no theories at all about these things. I'm here just to find out the truth—why this thing was built."

"Admirable," Barker said, and the coolness of his comment was lost in the colder wind. "Might I ask just what this device is?"

"Chronostasis temporal-recorder." He opened the legs and stood the machine next to the Altar Stone. "My team at MIT worked it up. We found that temporal movement—other than the usual twenty-four hours into the future every day—is instant death for anything living. At least we killed off roaches, rats, and chickens; there were no human volunteers. But inanimate objects can be moved without damage."

"Time travel?" Barker said in what he hoped was a diffident voice.

"Not really, time stasis would be a better description. The machine stands still and lets everything else move by it. We've penetrated a good ten thousand years into the past this way."

"If the machine stands still—that means that time is running backwards?"

"Perhaps it is; would you be able to tell the difference? Here, I think we're ready to go now."

Lanning adjusted the controls on the side of the machine, pressed a stud, then stepped back. A rapid whirring came from the depths of the device: Barker raised one quizzical eyebrow.

"A timer," Lanning explained. "It's not safe to be close to the thing when it's operating."

The whirring ceased and was followed by a shark click, immediately after which the entire apparatus vanished.

"This won't take long," Lanning said, and the machine reappeared even as he spoke. A glossy photograph dropped from a slot into his hand when he touched the back. He showed it to Barker.

"Just a trial run, I sent it back twenty minutes."

Although the camera had been pointing at them, the

two men were not in the picture. Instead, in darkish pastels due to the failing light, the photograph showed a view down the Avenue, with their parked truck just a tiny square in the distance. From the rear doors of the vehicle the two men could be seen removing the yellow box.

"That's very . . . impressive," Barker said, shocked into admission of the truth. "How far back can you send it?"

"Seems to be no limit, just depends on the power source. This model has nicad batteries and is good back to about ten thousand B.C."

"And the future?"

"A closed book, I'm afraid, but we may lick that problem yet." He extracted a small notebook from his hip pocket and consulted it, then set the dials once again. "These are the optimum dates, about the time we figure Stonehenge was built. I'm making this a multiple shot. This lever records the setting, so now I can feed in another one."

There were over twenty settings to be made, which necessitated a great deal of dial spinning. When it was finally done Lanning actuated the timer and went to join Barker.

This time the departure of the chronostasis temporal-recorder was much more dramatic. It vanished readily enough, but left a glowing replica of itself behind, a shimmering golden outline easily visible in the growing darkness.

"Is that normal?" Barker asked.

"Yes, but only on the big time jumps. No one is really sure just what it is, but we call it a temporal echo, the theory being that it is sort of a resonance in time caused by the sudden departure of the machine. It fades away in a couple of minutes."

Before the golden glow was completely gone the device itself returned, appearing solidly in place of its spectral echo. Lanning rubbed his hands together, then pressed the print button. The machine clattered in response and extruded a long strip of connected prints.

"Not as good as I expected," Lanning said. "We hit the daytime all right, but there is nothing much going on."

There was enough going on to almost stop Barker's archeologist heart. Picture after picture of the megalith standing strong and *complete,* the menhirs upright and the lintels in place upon all the sarsen stones.

"Lots of rock," Lanning said, "but no sign of the people who built the thing. Looks like someone's theories are wrong. Do you have any idea when it was put up?"

"Sir J. Norman Lockyer believed that it was erected on June twenty-fourth, sixteen eighty B.C.," he said abstractedly, still petrified by the photographs.

"Sounds good to me."

The dials were spun and the machine vanished once again. The picture this time was far more dramatic. A group of men in rough homespun genuflected, arms outstretched, facing toward the camera.

"We've got it now," Lanning chortled, and spun the machine about in a half circle so it faced in the opposite direction. "Whatever they're worshiping is behind the camera. I'll take a shot of it and we'll have a good idea why they built this thing."

The second picture was almost identical with the first, as were two more taken at right angles to the first ones.

"This is crazy," Lanning said, "they're all facing into the camera and bowing. Why—the machine must be sitting on top of whatever they are looking at."

"No, the angle proves that the tripod is on the same level that they are." Sudden realization hit Barker and his jaw sagged. "Is it possible that your temporal echo could be visible in the past as well?"

"Well . . . I don't see why not. Do you mean . . . ?"

"Correct. The golden glow of the machine caused by all those stops must have been visible on and off for years. It gave me a jolt when I first saw it and it must have been much more impressive to the people then."

"It fits," Lanning said, smiling happily and beginning to repack the machine. "They built Stonehenge around the image of the device sent back to see why they built Stonehenge. That's one problem solved."

"Solved! The problem has just begun. It's a paradox. Which of them, the machine or the monument, *came first?*"

Slowly, the smile faded from Dr. Lanning's face.

INCIDENT IN THE IND

"Thank God *that's* done." Adriann DuBois's voice bounced harshly from the tiled walls of the subway passage, punctuated by the sharp clack-clack of her high stiletto heels. There was a rattling rumble as an express train rushed through the station ahead and a wave of musty air washed over them.

"It's after one A.M.," Chester said and yawned widely and pressed the back of his hand to his mouth. "We'll probably have to wait an hour for a train."

"Don't be so negative, Chester," she said, and her voice had the same metallic ring as her heelsteps. "All the copy is finished now for the new account, we'll probably get a bonus, and we can take most of the day off tomorrow. Think positive like that and you'll feel a lot better, I assure you."

They reached the turnstile at that moment, before Chester could think of a snappy answer that didn't reek too much of one o'clock in the morning, and he fumbled a token into the slot. Adriann swept through as he probed deeper into his change pocket and discovered that this had been his last token. He turned wearily back to the change booth and muttered two or three good, dirty words under his breath.

"How many?" a voice mumbled from the dimness of the barred steel cell.

"Two, please." He slipped the change in through the tiny window. It wasn't that he minded paying her damn fare, after all she was a woman, but he wished she would at least say thanks or even nod her head to show that she didn't get into subways by divine right. After all they both worked in the same nut factory and earned the same money, and now she would be earning more. He had forgotten that last little fact for a moment. The slot swallowed his token and went "chunk" as he pushed through.

"I take the last car," Adriann said, squinting nearsightedly down the dark and empty tunnel. "Let's walk back to the end of the platform."

"I need the middle of the train," Chester said, but had to trot after her. Adriann never heard what she didn't need to hear.

"There's something I can tell you now, Chester," she began in her brisk man-to-man voice. "I couldn't really mention this before, since we both were doing the same work and in one sense competing for position. But since Blaisdell's coronary will have him out for a couple of weeks I'll be acting copy chief, with some more money to match—"

"I heard from the latrine grapevine. Congrats—"

"—so I'm in a position to pass on a bit of good advice to you. You have to push more, Chester, grab onto things when they come along . . ."

"For chrissake, Adriann, you sound like a bad commercial for crowded streetcars."

"And that sort of thing too. Little jokes. People begin to think you don't take your work seriously and that is sure death in the ad business."

"Of course I don't take the work seriously—who in their right mind could?" He heard a rumbling and looked, but the tunnel was still empty; it must have been a truck in the street above. "Are you going to tell me that you really *care* about writing deathless prose about milady's armpits smelling the right way from the use of the right Stink-Go-Way?"

"Don't be vulgar, Chester; you know you can be sweet when you want to," she said, taking advantage of female reasoning to ignore his arguments and to inject a note of emotion into a previously logical conversation.

"You're damn right I can be sweet," he said huskily, not adverse to a little emotion himself. With her mouth shut Adriann was pretty attractive in a past-thirtyish way. The knitted dress did wonders for her bottom, and undoubtedly the foundation-maker's artifice had something to do with the outstanding attraction of her frontpiece, but more in underpinning than in padding, he was willing to bet.

He shuffled close and slipped his arms around her waist and patted lightly on the top of her flank. "I can be sweet and I can remember a time when you didn't mind being sweet right back."

"That's a long time finished, boy," she said in her schoolmarm voice and peeled his arms away with a picking-up-worms expression. Chester's newspaper fell out from under his arm, where he had stuffed it, and he bent over mumbling to pick it up from the gritty platform.

She was quiet for a moment after this, twisting her skirt around a bit and rubbing out the wrinkles as if brushing away the contamination of his touch. There were no sounds from the street overhead, and the long, dimly lit station was as silent as a burial vault. They were alone with the strange loneliness that can be experienced only in a large city, of people somewhere always close by, yet always cut off. Tired, suddenly depressed, Chester lit a cigarette and inhaled deeply.

"You're not allowed to smoke in the subway," Adriann said with detached coldness.

"I'm not allowed to smoke, nor to give you a little squeeze, to make jokes in the office, or to look with justified contempt at our current client."

"No you're not," she snapped and leveled a delicate finger with a blood-red nail at him. "And since you brought it up, I'll tell you something else. Other people in the office have noticed it too, and this I *know*. You have been with the firm longer than I, so they considered you for the copy chief's job—and turned you down. And I was told in utmost confidence that they are actually considering letting you go. Does that mean anything to you?"

"It does. It means I have been nursing a viper in my bosom. I seem to remember that I got you this job and even had to convince old Blaisdell that you could do the work. You acted right grateful too, at the time—remember those passionate scenes in the foyer of your boardinghouse?"

"Don't be a pig!"

"Now the passion is dead, so is any chance of a raise,

and it looks like my job is out the window as well. With dear Adriann for a friend, who needs an enemy . . ."

"There are things living in the subway, you know."

The voice was husky and trembled, it came suddenly from behind them, from what they thought was the empty platform, startling them both. Adriann gasped and turned quickly. There was a pool of darkness next to the large litter bin and neither of them had noticed the man slumped against the wall, seated there. He struggled to his feet and stepped forward.

"How dare you!" Adriann said shrilly, startled and angry. "Hiding there, eavesdropping on a private conversation. Aren't there any police in this subway?"

"There are *things,* you know," the man said, ignoring her, grinning up at Chester, his head twisted to one side.

He was a bum, one of the crimpled horde that had splattered out over New York City when the Bowery elevated was torn down and light penetrated that clogged street of human refuse. Photophobes to a man, they stumbled away seeking dimmer illumination. For many of them the gloomed caverns of the subways offered refuge, heated cars in the winter, toilet facilities, panhandling prospects, quiet corners for collapsing. This one wore the uniform of his trade: shapeless, filthy pants with most of the fly buttons missing; crumpled jacket tied close with string, with a number of unusual undergarments visible at the open neck; shoes cracked, split, and flapping; darkened skin as wrinkled as a mummy's with a pencil line of dirt in every crack. His mouth was a black orifice, the few remaining teeth standing like stained tombstones in memory of their vanished brothers. Examined in detail the man was a revolting sight, but so commonplace to this city that he was as much a part of it as the wire trash basket and the steaming manholes.

"What kind of things?" Chester asked while he groped in his pocket for a dime to buy their freedom. Adriann turned her back on them both.

"*Things* that live in the earth," the bum said and smiled blearily, pressing a grimy finger to his lips. "People who know never talk about it. Don't want to frighten the tourists away, no they don't. Scales, claws, down here in the subway darkness."

"Give him some money—get rid of him—this is terrible!" Adriann said shrilly.

Chester dropped two nickels into the cupped hand, carefully, from a few inches above so he wouldn't have to touch the stained skin.

"What do these things do?" he asked, not because ho really cared what the man had to say, but to annoy Adriann, a touch of the old sadist nudging him on.

The bum rubbed the nickels together in his palm. "They live here, hiding, looking out, that's what they do. You should give them something when you're alone, late at night like this, staying near the end of the platform. Pennies are good, just put them down there at the edge where they can reach up and get them. Dimes good too, but no nickels like you gave me."

"You're hearing a very fancy panhandle story," Adriann said, angry now that her first fright had gone. "Now get away from that old tramp."

"Why only pennies and dimes?" Chester asked, interested in spite of himself. It *was* very black over the edge of the platform: anything could be hiding there.

"Pennies because they like peanuts, they work the machines with pennies when no one is around. And dimes for the coke machines, they drink that sometimes instead of water. I've seen them . . ."

"I'm going for a policeman," Adriann snorted and click-clacked away, but stopped after she had gone about ten yards. Both men ignored her.

"Come on now," Chester smiled at the bum, who was running trembling fingers through his matted hair, "you can't expect me to believe that. If these things eat only peanuts there is no reason to buy them off—"

"I didn't say that was all they ate!" The grimy hand locked on Chester's sleeve before he could move away, and he recoiled from the man's breath as he leaned close to whisper. "What they really like to eat is *people*, but they won't bother you as long as you leave them a little something. Would you like to see one?"

"After this buildup I certainly would."

The bum tottered over to the waste-paper receptacle, big as a trunk on end, olive drab metal with two flap doors in the hatlike cover.

"Now you just gotta take a quick look because they don't like to be looked at," the man said and gave one of the flaps a push in and let go.

Chester stepped back, startled. He had had only a glimpse, had he really seen two glowing red spots in there, a foot apart, monstrous eyes? Could there be—no the whole thing was just too damn silly. There was the distant rumble of a train.

"Great show, Dad," he said, and dropped some pennies near the edge of the platform. "That'll keep them in peanuts for a while." He walked quickly down to Adriann. "The spiel got better after you left; the old buzzard swears that one of the things is hiding there in the trash can. So I left a bribe—just in case."

"How can you be so stupid—"

"You're tired, dear—and your claws are showing. And you're being repetitive as well."

The train rattled closer, sweeping a cloud of dead air before it. Musty air, almost like the smell of an animal . . . he had never noticed that before.

"You are stupid—and superstitious," she had to raise her voice above the roar of the approaching train. "You're the kind of person who knocks on wood and won't step on cracks and worries about black cats."

"I sure am, because it doesn't hurt. There's enough bad luck around as it is without looking for any more. There probably isn't a *thing* in that trash can—but I'm not going to put my arm in there to find out."

"You're a simple-minded child."

"Oh, am I!" They were both shouting now to be heard above the train that was rocking by next to them, brakes squealing to a stop. "Well let's see you put *your* arm in there if you are so damn smart."

"Childish!"

It was late and Chester was tired and his temper was frayed. The train shuddered to a halt behind him. He ran toward the end of the platform, digging in his pocket and pulling out all of his loose change.

"Here," he shouted, pushing the flap of the waste bin in an inch and pouring the coins through the gap. "Money. Plenty dimes, pennies. Plenty cokes, peanuts. You grab and eat next person who comes here."

Behind him Adriann was laughing. The train doors shooshed open and the old bum shuffled into the car.

"That's your Queens train," Adriann said, still laughing. "Better take it before the *things* get you. I'm waiting for the uptown local."

"Take this," he said, still angry, holding out his newspaper to her. "This is so funny, you're not superstitious—let's see you put this in the basket." He jumped for the train doors, catching them just as they closed.

"Of course, darling," she called, her face red from laughing. "And I'll tell the office about it tomorrow—" the doors slid shut cutting off the rest of her words.

The train shuddered a bit and started to move. Through the dirt-stained glass he saw her walk to the waste container and shove the paper in through the flap. One of the pillars came between them as the train picked up speed.

Then he saw her again and she still had her hand to the lid—or had she poked her arm in up to the elbow?—it was hard to tell through the dirty glass. Then another pillar, they were beginning to flicker by. Another glimpse and with the blurred window and the bad light he couldn't be sure but it looked as if she was bent over and had poked her head into the opening.

This window was no good. He ran the few steps to the rear of the car where a larger—and somewhat cleaner—window was set into the rear door. The train was halfway down the platform now, swaying as it picked up speed and he had a last glimpse of her before the row of pillars merged into a blur that cut off vision completely.

She couldn't possibly be halfway into that container, the flapped opening certainly wasn't big enough for a person to get through. Yet how else to explain that he had seen just her skirt and legs sticking out, wiggling wildly in the air?

Of course it had been only a blurred glimpse and he was mistaken. He turned back to the empty car—no, not empty. The bum slumped in a seat, already asleep.

The ragged man looked up at Chester, gave him a quick, secretive grin, then closed his eyes again. Chester went to the other end of the car and sat down. He yawned and scrunched lower.

He could doze until they reached his station; he always woke up in time.

It would be nice if the copy chief's job was still open; he could use the extra money.

IF

"We are there; we are correct. The computations were perfect. That is the place below."

"You are a worm," 17 said to her companion, 35, who resembled her every way other than in number. "That is the place. But nine years too early. Look at the meter."

"I am a worm. I shall free you of the burden of my useless presence." 35 removed her knife from the scabbard and tested the edge, which proved to be exceedingly sharp. She placed it against the white wattled width of her neck and prepared to cut her throat.

"Not now," 17 hissed. "We are shorthanded already and your corpse would be valueless to this expedition. Get us to the correct time at once. Our power is limited, you may remember."

"It shall be done as you command," 35 said as she slithered to the bank of controls. 44 ignored the talk, keeping her multicell eyes focused on the power control bank, constantly making adjustments with her spatulate fingers in response to the manifold dials.

"That is it," 17 announced, rasping her hands together with pleasure. "The correct time, the correct place. We must descend and make our destiny. Give praise to the Saur of All, who rules the destinies of all."

"Praise Saur," her two companions muttered, all of their attention on the controls.

Straight down from the blue sky the globular vehicle fell. It was round and featureless, save for the large rectangular port, on the bottom now, and made of some sort of green metal, perhaps anodized aluminum, though it looked harder. It had no visible means of flight or support, yet it fell at a steady and controlled rate. Slower and

131

slower it moved until it dropped from sight behind the ridge at the northern end of Johnson's Lake, just at the edge of the tall pine grove. There were fields nearby, with cows, who did not appear at all disturbed by the visitor. No human being was in sight to view the landing. A path cut in from the lake here, a scuffed dirt trail that went to the highway.

An oriole sat on a bush and warbled sweetly; a small rabbit hopped from the field to nibble a stem of grass. This bucolic and peaceful scene was interrupted by the scuff of feet down the trail and a high-pitched and singularly monotonous whistling. The bird flew away, a touch of soundless color, while the rabbit disappeared into the hedge. A boy came over the rise from the direction of the lake shore. He wore ordinary boy clothes and carried a schoolbag in one hand, a small and homemade cage of wire screen in the other. In the cage was a small lizard, which clung to the screen, its eyes rolling in what presumably was fear. The boy, whistling shrilly, trudged along the path and into the shade of the pine grove.

"Boy," a high-pitched and tremulous voice called out. "Can you hear me, boy?"

"I certainly can," the boy said, stopping and looking around for the unseen speaker. "Where are you?"

"I am by your side, but I am invisible. I am your fairy godmother . . ."

The boy made a rude sound by sticking out his tongue and blowing across it while it vibrated. "I don't believe in invisibility or fairy godmothers. Come out of those woods, whoever you are."

"All boys believe in fairy godmothers," the voice said, but a worried tone edged the words now. "I know all kinds of secrets. I know your name is Don and . . ."

"Everyone knows my name is Don and no one believes any more in fairies. Boys now believe in rockets, submarines, and atomic energy."

"Would you believe space travel?"

"I would."

Slightly relieved, the voice came on stronger and deeper. "I did not wish to frighten you, but I am really from Mars and have just landed . . ."

Don made the rude noise again. "Mars has no atmosphere and no observable forms of life. Now come out of there and stop playing games."

After a long silence the voice said, "Would you consider time travel?"

"I could. Are you going to tell me that you are from the future?"

With relief: "Yes I am."

"Then come out where I can see you."

"There are some things that the human eye should not look upon . . ."

"Horseapples! The human eye is okay for looking at anything you want to name. You come out of there so I can see who you are—or I'm leaving."

"It is not advisable." The voice was exasperated. "I can prove I am a temporal traveler by telling you the answers to tomorrow's mathematics test. Wouldn't that be nice? Number one, 1.76. Number two . . ."

"I don't like to cheat, and even if I did you can't cheat on the new math. Either you know it or you fail it. I'm going to count to ten, then go."

"No, you cannot! I must ask you a favor. Release that common lizard you have trapped and I will give you three wishes—I mean, answer three questions."

"Why should I let it go?"

"Is that the first of your questions?"

"No. I want to know what's going on before I do anything. This lizard is special. I never saw another one like it around here."

"You are right. It is an Old World acrodont lizard of the order Rhiptoglossa, commonly called a chameleon."

"It *is!*" Don was really interested now. He squatted in the path and took a red-covered book from his schoolbag and laid it on the ground. He turned the cage until the lizard was on the bottom and placed it carefully on the book. "Will it really turn color?"

"To an observable amount, yes. Now if you release her . . ."

"How do you know it's a her? The time-traveler bit again?"

"If you must know, yes. The creature was purchased from a pet store by one Jim Benan, and is one of a pair. They were both released two days ago when Benan, deranged by the voluntary drinking of a liquid containing quantities of ethyl alcohol, sat on the cage. The other, unfortunately, died of his wounds, and this one alone survives. The release . . ."

"I think this whole thing is a joke and I'm going home now. Unless you come out of there so I can see who you are."

"I warn you . . ."

"Good-bye." Don picked up the cage. "Hey, she turned sort of brick red!"

"Do not leave. I will come forth."

Don looked on, with a great deal of interest, while the creature walked out from between the trees. It was blue, had large and goggling—independently moving—eyes, wore a neatly cut brown jumpsuit, and had a pack slung on its back. It was also only about seven inches tall.

"You don't much look like a man from the future," Don said. "In fact you don't look like a man at all. You're too small."

"I might say that you are too big: size is a matter of relevancy. And I am from the future, though I am not a man."

"That's for sure. In fact you look a lot like a lizard." In sudden inspiration, Don looked back and forth at the traveler and at the cage. "In fact you look a good deal like this chameleon here. What's the connection?"

"That is not to be revealed. You will now do as I command or I will injure you gravely." 17 turned and waved toward the woods. "35, this is an order. Appear and destroy that growth over there."

Don looked on with increasing interest as the green basketball of metal drifted into sight from under the trees. A circular disk slipped away on one side and a gleaming nozzle, not unlike the hose nozzle on a toy firetruck, appeared through the opening. It pointed toward a hedge a good thirty feet away. A shrill whining began from the depths of the sphere, rising in pitch until it was almost inaudible. Then, suddenly, a thin line of light spat out toward the shrub, which crackled and instantly burst into flame. Within a second it was a blackened skeleton.

"The device is called a roxidizer, and is deadly," 17

said. "Release the chameleon at once or we will turn it on you."

Don scowled. "All right. Who wants the old lizard anyway." He put the cage on the ground and started to open the cover. Then he stopped—and sniffed. Picking up the cage again he started across the grass toward the blackened bush.

"Come back!" 17 screeched. "We will fire if you go another step."

Don ignored the lizardoid, which was now dancing up and down in an agony of frustration, and ran to the bush. He put his hand out—and apparently right through the charred stems.

"I thought something was fishy," he said. "All that burning and everything just upwind of me—and I couldn't smell a thing." He turned to look at the time traveler, who was slumped in gloomy silence. "It's just a projected image of some kind, isn't it? Some kind of three-dimensional movie." He stopped in sudden thought, then walked over to the still hovering temporal transporter. When he poked at it with his finger he apparently pushed his hand right into it.

"And this thing isn't here either. Are you?"

"There is no need to experiment. I, and our ship, are present only as what might be called temporal echoes. Matter cannot be moved through time, that is an impossibility, but the concept of matter can be temporally projected. I am sure that this is too technical for you . . ."

"You're doing great so far. Carry on."

"Our projections are here in a real sense to us, though we can only be an image or a sound wave to any observers in the time we visit. Immense amounts of energy are required and almost the total resources of our civilization are involved in this time transfer."

"Why? And the truth for a change. No more fairy god-mother and that kind of malarkey."

"I regret the necessity to use subterfuge, but the secret is too important to reveal casually without attempting other means of persuasion."

"Now we get to the real story." Don sat down and crossed his legs comfortably. "Give."

"We need your aid, or our very society is threatened. Very recently—on our time scale—strange disturbances were detected by our instruments. Ours is a simple saurian existence, some million or so years in the future, and our race is dominant. Yours has long since vanished in a manner too horrible to mention to your young ears. Something is threatening our entire race and research quickly uncovered the fact that we are about to be overwhelmed by a probability wave and wiped out, a great wave of negation sweeping toward us from our remote past."

"You wouldn't mind tipping me off to what a probability wave is, would you?"

"I will take an example from your own literature. If your grandfather had died without marrying, you would not have been born and would not now exist."

"But I do."

"The matter is debatable in the greater xan-probility universe, but we shall not discuss that now. Our power is limited. To put the affair simply, we traced our ancestral lines back through all the various mutations and changes until we found the individual protolizard from which our line sprung."

"Let me guess." Don pointed at the cage. "This is the one?"

"She is." 17 spoke in solemn tones, as befitted the moment. "Just as somewhen, somewhere there is a prototarsier from which your race sprung, so is there this temporal mother of ours. She will bear young soon, and they will breed and grow in this pleasant valley. The rocks near the lake have an appreciable amount of radioactivity, which will cause mutations. The centuries will roll by and, one day, our race will reach its heights of glory.

"But not if you don't open that cage."

Don rested his chin on fist and thought. "You're not putting me on anymore? This is the truth?"

17 drew herself up and waved both arms—or front legs—over her head. "By the Saur of All, I promise," she intoned. "By the stars eternal, the seasons vernal, the clouds, the sky, the matriarchal I . . ."

"Just cross your heart and hope to die, that will be good enough for me."

The lizardoid moved its eyes in concentric circles and performed this ritual.

"Okay then, I'm as softhearted as the next guy when it comes to wiping out whole races."

Don unbent the piece of wire that sealed the cage and opened the top. The chameleon rolled one eye up at him and looked at the opening with the other. 17 watched in awed silence and the time vehicle bobbed closer.

"Get going," Don said, and shook the lizard out into the grass.

This time the chameleon took the hint and scuttled away among the bushes, vanishing from sight.

"That takes care of the future," Don said. "Or the past from your point of view."

17 and the time machine vanished silently and Don was alone again on the path.

"Well you could of at least said thanks before taking off like that. People have more manners than lizards any day, I'll tell you that."

He picked up the now-empty cage and his schoolbag and started for home.

He had not heard the quick rustle in the bushes, nor did he see the prowling tomcat with the limp chameleon in its jaws.

CONTACT MAN

"You will leave the air lock and you will look for trouble," the captain said. "You are carrying enough armament to start a small war—and that is just what you are expected to do. Get out there and stir things up . . ."

"How about my stirring up your guts to begin with, Cap," Chesney said, swinging up the laseray with a lightning motion in spite of his heavy pressure suit. He centered it on the Captain's midriff and squeezed the trigger. The gun clicked loudly.

"Save your combative spirit for the outside," the captain said coldly. "What happens then is up to you. There is no food and a very limited supply of water in your suit. You will stay out there until you have done the job correctly. You must satisfy me, for I, and I alone, will be your judge. If you do a bad job or no job I'll just leave you out there to die and rot in that armored suit. Just think that you're wearing a ready-made tomb, and that I'm the only man who can get you out of it. Satisfy me, Chesney."

Chesney cursed him loudly and fluently, but the captain didn't bother to listen.

"Put him out," the captain said, and two ratings grabbed Chesney's arms and pushed him into the open air lock.

"You're asking me to commit suicide," Chesney said as the lock began to close. "Who gave you the right to kill me?"

"You did, Chesney, when you rebeled against the Admiral-Emperor. And the courts gave it to me when they judged you guilty of treason and sentenced you to death.

It was your choice to volunteer for this work instead of accepting the death penalty . . ."

Chesney stopped listening. The inner lock was almost closed—but there was still enough of a gap to roll a grenade through! He groped at his right hip, where there was a satchel of grenades—labeled thoughtfully with the red cross of death—but it was locked tight and he could not open it. The inner lock thudded home and was secured and, with grinding slowness the outer lock began to open. The captain's voice sounded from the speaker inside his helmet and he could neither silence it nor escape it.

"These are my orders. You will leave the ship at once. You will follow a course of thirty-two on the radio-compass repeater on your wrist. You will quickly come to a village of the natives of this planet. You will do your best to destroy that village. I will be watching and listening, and I warn you, it had better be your best."

As soon as the opening was wide enough, Chesney hurled himself through it, the weight of his armor and equipment crashing him heavily to the ground. Yet it was a controlled fall, because as he hit he was diving forward, rolling and twisting so that when he came to his feet again he was facing back toward the ship and—once again—squeezing futilely on the laseray's trigger. The mechanism of the incredibly powerful weapon emitted a mocking click. The unceasing voice drummed in his ears.

". . . get in there and shoot up anything that looks interesting, and the more interesting it looks the more you're going to shoot it up. The natives of this filthy piece of rock appear to be harmless primitives, but we've run into that before."

As the outer lock closed and sealed shut, the laseray came to life in his hands and his helmet opaqued automatically as the burning beam of laser light sprang out. It tore a gaping, burning trench in the ground and he pulled up on the gun so that the actinic fury seared up the side of the spaceship and splashed from the control room ports high above the ground. The voice rang in his helmet with cold fury.

"How stupid a man are you, Chesney? Can you imagine for an instant that we would arm you with anything that could possibly harm this ship? Inside the ship, yes, that is why we activate your armory by remote after you have left. But this spacer is armored to withstand anything short of an H bomb. Fool! You try my patience and I am tempted to blast you where you stand. I won't. I want this mission done. But I tell you—and this is truth, not warning—that you are halfway to failure now. If you do a fair job, I will leave you here. If you do a good job, I will leave you here. If you do a most excellent job, I might possibly consider taking you back aboard. Now move!"

A man cannot argue with facts, only with other people. Chesney had discovered that many years earlier. The captain was a fact of life and death, or rather death and death; he recognized that now. Spinning about he put his back to the ship and tried to forget about it. With a quick and sweeping motion he checked that the cover on the grenade satchel was unlocked, his knife free in its leg sheath, that all of his armory of violence was in operating order. Looking at the repeater compass he turned about until the needle touched 32, then triggered his jetpack. It roared to life, the harness kicked him under the arms, and he was airborne.

He had to alter course occasionally to avoid the weird structures that littered the landscape, but he barely glanced at them, keeping his attention focused ahead. The captain had said that—for all their artificial look—they were a natural phenomenon, and he took the captain at his word. At least in this. The captain would not lie about anything that affected his survival.

A valley opened ahead filled with the beehivelike structures that had been described to him, the village. Almost automatically he dropped lower to take cover and the hated voice roared in his ears.

"Stay high. Go in fast. Hit like lightening. Hit like the wrath of hell. That is the way you will do it."

"I wish I were doing it to you," he shouted as he arced high and dropped with his laseray flaming.

It speared through the dwellings as though they were paper, tearing and rending and collapsing them into smoking rubble. The natives poured out like ants from a disturbed nest and the flaring death cut through their ranks just as easily. As he dropped down he saw how they fell and died, kicking their many slate-gray limbs.

"They're just aborigines," he raged, though he never ceased firing. "They are helpless, simple, and stupid —look there. Those, the ones I just burned, they were armed with stone knives and rock hammers. This is murder—worse, senseless slaughter."

Yet, even while he shouted he landed and fired about him in a circle, cutting down all who attacked. And attack they did, in a furious, helpless mob. Running into the burning arms of destruction.

"Yes, they do look simple," the calm voice spoke into his ears, "but we've seen that ruse before. Keep doing your work. Stop if you dare, for a second only, and I will judge you as having failed."

Chesney's voice cursed the slaughter, while his body worked industriously to wreak it.

"Killers, we're all killers," he screeched and burnt down a group that had been attacking behind the tissue-paper defenses of crude shields.

"We sow death and one day our race will reap the harvest," he shouted as he incinerated a large building and all who had sheltered within it.

"I'll not be a part of this—a race that does this deserves to be blotted from the universe," he gasped as he found an open lane of fire and killed hundreds.

The laseray died abruptly and a red light blinked on inside his helmet, indicating that the weapon was overheating and the safeties had switched it off. But at the instant the light appeared he had slung the weapon and hurled two grenades, triggering the jetpack at the same time. He was aloft as they exploded, dropping others in a trail of death as he went.

"Turn to heading eighty-seven," the captain said. "Wake things up over there."

"The buildings look skimpy there, the bigger, more important-looking ones are in the other direction . . ."

"You act; I think!" the voice roared. "I am intelligence, you are animal. Go!" But Chesney was already on his way and the voice continued, slightly pacified. "Thoughts have patterns, as do all things. If the pattern here is misdirection and those creatures aren't as simple as they seem, then there will be more misdirection. We examine the unimportant."

"A waste of life, a waste of everything—even these grenades," Chesney said as he rained explosive death on the constructions below. A single grenade for each hovel, disintegrating it, for the grenades were designed to be used against stronger structures. "What way is this to make contact with a new world, a new race?"

"The way we have chosen and the way we must go on," the ruthless voice said. "The human race is now at war with the entire galaxy. When a new planet is found—such as this one—its inhabitants can be only subjects or enemies. There are no neutrals in this battle. We have no time—nor do we have the inclination—to be sociable. Therefore this simple means of contact, with only one man's life at stake, a worthless life like yours. You kill and keep killing. If the natives of this ugly planet are as simple as they look you will kill enough to prove it, and they will become the newest subject race to serve the Admiral-Emperor. They will quickly breed back the individuals you have slaughtered, but will never breed out the memory of our wrath. We will remind them occasionally. They will serve us well."

"Let me stop then. Enslave them. Let me cease killing."

"No. I am not satisfied. They die too easily. If this is an advanced race we must wage war on them quickly, local and destructive war before they unite with our enemies. Move on. Destroy."

"There are few buildings. It is hard to find a target," Chesney said, soaring high and aiming each grenade well. The constructions were few, and widely scattered.

"Yet this area is flat and appears as well located as the others," the captain mused. "Why the barrenness unless to mislead us?"

"You suspect deceit and treachery because you are deceitful and treacherous," Chesney shouted.

"Of course," the captain's voice spoke calmly, "that is why I have been chosen for this work. Go. The building there, the isolated one at a bearing of twenty-seven on your repeater. Blow it up, then place a second grenade exactly in the center of the first grenade's crater, then land."

"It's dangerous," Chesney said as he sank through the yellow haze of smoke into the newly blasted pit. "The dirt is crumbling. I could be trapped here."

"I do not care. Do as directed. Kick your right toe deep into the soft earth, until it is buried. It contains a delicate seismograph. Now plant your feet firmly and balance yourself well. *Do not move your feet again until you have permission.* I am unlocking the clamps on the instrument. It is now functional. If you move you will destroy it and I will kill you. Did I tell you the suit contains a lethal device that I control?" The captain's laugh was completely humorless, and Chesney cursed him in a weary monotone.

"Now we are ready," the captain said. "Unsling your grenade launcher—*slowly, fool!* Concussion grenade, contact fuse, range one kilometer. Fire."

Chesney did, and as the missile screamed up from the crater a hissing crowd of aliens poured over the edge. Chesney could dimly hear their sibilant screams through his armored suit. "I am under attack," he said.

"Do not move or defend yourself," the captain ordered. A rapid series of clicks echoed inside the suit. "I have sealed and disarmed your weapons so they cannot turn them against you."

A distant thud sounded as the aliens attacked. Slate-gray flesh plastered itself against his transparent faceplate and orange teeth clattered on its surface. Stone weapons beat at his armor. He shrank down inside the suit, but did not move.

"This close . . . they repel me," he said. "They are . . . loathsome, incredibly so . . ."

"Do not move, the seismic echoes arrive and the computer is processing them." A moment's silence, then: "Oh, good, very, very good!" There was a trace of emotion, almost joy in the captain's voice. "Your laseray!" he shouted. "It is activated. Turn it on the crater wall, your suit will not be affected by the reflected radiation."

But the aliens were seared, charred, destroyed in a moment. They melted from sight leaving only carbon imprints on the suit as memory of their existence.

"Jetpack, course nineteen," the captain ordered, and Chesney rose clear of the ground and raced above it. "Be ready to cut off . . . *now!* Land here. Place and disarm your atomic device."

His chest pack whirred and deposited a heavy, shining gray ovoid in his hands. He knelt and put it carefully down before him, settling it into an impression he scraped in the sandy ground. Slowly, steadily, he turned the black knob on the top, then pulled out the knob and the oily strand of black wire attached to it. He felt a click and a steady hum through his fingertips and he shivered.

"Leave," the voice commanded, and he was airborne at maximum lift with the harness tearing a pleasing pain into his armpits as he was carried away from the egg of death.

"Course thirty-five," the voice directed. "There is a high bank at the river there that you will shelter behind. There—descend now. Set your jets at cancel-G. Stay in the blast shadow of the bank. Do not touch the ground, the ground wave will be strong here. Good. Face away from the atomic device. Opaque your helmet. Raise your arm before your faceplate. Close your eyes. Are you ready?"

"Ready . . ."

But before the last syllable left his lips the world exploded and he was aware of the scream of universe-filling flame despite his dark barriers. The ground heaved, the tortured atmosphere boiled, great waves churned and fought in the water below.

"Be ready," the voice directed. "The fireball is almost by. Now—*blast!* Cross ground zero at maximum speed, your suit is radiationproof. Look at the crater at all times; this will direct the camera in your suit."

Chesney was on his way before the order was complete. Above him the rising flame-cloud boiled, and below was the glowing mouth of hell. He passed between the two and the temperature in his suit rose instantly until the metal burned where it touched his body, and he shrank from this and from the flood of invisible radiation he knew was hurtling toward him. Through pain and fear some portion of obedience or terrible curiosity kept his eyes turned toward the crater below. Through the crackle of static the captain's voice trickled in.

"Something big down there, large and bulky. Natural perhaps, but we will see now."

All was blackness through the opaqued helmet, except for the glowing core of fire below. Was there some kind of form to it, some linear structure there beneath the ground?

"I was right!" the captain roared. "We are under attack, strong attack. Wonderful! Energy weapons of immense strength. I am taking off . . ."

"Don't abandon me!" Chesney shouted as something exploded against his leg and pain tore through him. "They are firing on me too."

"Course one forty-five," the captain said. "Blast at maximum power for six seconds, then ground. This ship will land at the same time with the airlock open. We will stay grounded for exactly two seconds, no longer. We will leave whether you are in the dock or not. I am being very generous."

Chesney did not answer because it took all of his strength to stay conscious despite the pain in his wounded body, blood ran down his chin from his teeth sunk deep into his lower lip, and all of his fading consciousness was focused on his radio-compass repeater and his chronometer.

At the end of the sixth second he cut the blast and hit the ground, rolling end over end until the thick foliage slowed and stopped. He did not struggle to free himself but triggered his laseray and burned himself free.

The spacer was dropping, almost on top of him, the smoke of its jets engulfing him. Before it touched he was jumping toward it, plunging headfirst into the waiting black opening of the open airlock.

It was a very close thing. He was in the air, in the lock, when the ship took off and the floor came up and smashed him at last into the blissful no-pain of unconsciousness.

"They were very obstinate," the captain said. "They kept fighting too long and the battle was becoming wasteful. So we had to drop a planet buster and the planet is still afire. A waste."

"Do you care?" Chesney asked, his voice muffled by the brace that held his broken jaw. Antipain drugs canceled his awareness of most of his burned and broken body, wrapped heavily with bandages. His bloodstream also contained many antiradiation drugs since the captain had lied a little about the radiationproofing of his suit.

"Do I care?" the captain thought for a moment. "I really don't know if I do anymore. When one does the work, one becomes the work. The human animal is very adaptable. Once, like you, I cared, but that was a very long time ago."

The drugs could not cancel all the pain, and pain made Chesney aware of himself and he forgot the planet, now aflame, and its gray-skinned inhabitants, all dead.

"What happens to me now?" he asked.

The captain pointed to the floor. "When you survived you were automatically enrolled for life in the Space Navy of the Admiral-Emperor and will serve on a ship like this."

"I'll not be one of the hopeless creatures you have below decks . . ."

"Of course not. Having survived you will now be in control of one of these contact vessels. Congratulations, Captain." There was icy laughter in his voice.

"You lie!"

"I do not. If you survive ten missions you will be promoted to a higher position that is not quite as dangerous."

"That means . . ." Chesney had to marshal his thoughts against the pain and drugs. ". . . that means that you, too, not too long ago, were a contact man like myself?"

"Exactly. Seven missions ago. We are the same."

Chesney was shocked by the thought. "Can this mean that there is no hope of end to this tyranny? That all men are destined to die or join the battle?"

"It does," the captain said, and sighed ponderously. "I was sad for many days when I first realized it and I had my gun in my hand to kill myself, but I did not feel like dying just yet. You and I are the same and all mankind is doomed and there is nothing else to do. We keep destroying or we will be destroyed. Welcome."

"No!"

"Too late to say that. You chose when you left the ship and killed rather than be killed. Most men do."

"What happened? Why all this—all this?"

"No one will ever know. All of the past has been rewritten and all history is a lie. I have seen peaceful races, that we have enslaved of course, and I like to think that mankind was also peaceful at one time as well. Somehow, somewhere, sometime, violence was chosen as the answer to all problems. The violent men, the military men, took charge, and once in charge they stayed in charge. They will never relinquish their power."

"I am tired," Chesney said, his head falling forward.

"Have a drink with me first; then we will put you back in your bunk. The first time out is tiring."

They raised their glasses and the captain said, "Death to the enemy."

"We cannot say that," the other captain said.

"Because we are the enemy?"

"Of course."

They drank the toast anyway.

THE PAD

A STORY OF THE DAY AFTER THE DAY
AFTER TOMORROW

In the expansive, expensive atmosphere of Sardi's Topside, two hundred stories above the city, a pretty girl was no novelty, nor a beautiful one either for that matter. So the redhead in the green suit, who would certainly have drawn stares, turned heads, on the lower levels, received no attention here at all until she stopped at Ron Lowell-Stein's table and slapped him. A good, roundhouse smack right across the kisser.

His bodyguards, who now made up for their earlier inattention with an exaggerated display of muscle, grabbed her and squeezed her, and one even went so far as to push a gun against the base of her spine.

"Go ahead and have them kill me," she said, shaking her lovely, shoulder-length hair while an angry flush suffused the whiteness of her skin. "Add murder to your list of other crimes."

Ron, who rose at once because he was always polite to women, dismissed the bodyguards with a tilt of his head and said, "Would you care to sit down and tell me to which crimes you are referring?"

"Don't play the hypocrite with me, you juvenile Don Juan. I'm talking about my friend, Dolores, the girl whom you ruined."

"Is she ruined? I frankly thought she would be good for many years to come."

This time he caught her wrist before she could connect, proof that the years of polo, copter-hockey, and skeet shooting had toned his muscles and reflexes well. "It seems rather foolish to stand here like this. Can we not sit and fight in undertones like civilized people? I'll order Black Velvet—that is champagne and stout if you have never tried it—which is a great soother and nerve settler."

"I'll not sit with a man like you," she said as she sat down, firmly pressed into place by the strength of that polo-playing wrist.

"I am Ron Lowell-Stein, the man you hate, but you have not introduced yourself . . . ?"

"It's none of your damn business."

"Women should leave swearing to men, who do it so much better." He looked up as one of his bodyguards pulled a printed sheet from his pocketfax and handed it over. "Beatrice Carfax," he read. "I'll call you Bea since I have no liking for these classic names. Father . . . Mother . . . born . . . why you sweet thing, you are only twenty-two. Blood type O; occupation, dancer." His eyes jumped across to her, moved slowly down her torso. "I like that," he said, barely audibly. "Dancers have such beautifully muscled bodies."

She blushed again at the obviousness and pushed away the crystal beaker of dark and bubbling liquid that had been set before her, but he firmly slid it back.

"I do not feel that I have ruined your friend Dolores," he said. "In fact, I thought I was doing her a favor. However, because you are so attractive and forthright I shall give her fifty thousand dollars, a dowry that I know will unruin her in the eyes of any prospective husband."

Beatrice gasped at the sum. "You can't mean this."

"But I do. There is only one condition attached. That you have dinner with me tonight, after which we shall see a performance of the Yugoslavian State Ballet."

"Do you think that you can—work your will upon me?" she said hotly.

"Oh, goodness me," he said, touching his pristine handkerchief to the corners of his eyes. "I do not mean to laugh but I have not heard that phrase in, well, I have never heard it spoken aloud, to be exact. I like you, my Bea. You are one of nature's blessings with your sincere naïveté and round little bottom and my chauffeur will pick you up at seven. And, in answer to your question, I shall be frank with you, franker than with most girls who seem to expect some aura of romanticism, yes, I do expect to—work my will upon you."

"You cannot!"

"Fine, then you have nothing to fear. Please wear your gold sequin dress; I'm looking forward greatly to seeing you in it."

"What are you talking about? I don't own a gold dress."

"You do now. It will be delivered before you reach home."

Before she could protest the headwaiter appeared and said, *"Scusi mille,* Mr. Lowell-Stein, but your luncheon guests are here."

Two balding and rounded businessmen came up, Brazilians from the look of them, and as the men shook hands the bodyguards helped Bea to her feet and, with subtle pressures, moved her toward the exit. Preserving her dignity, with an effort, she shrugged away from them and made her own way out of the door. Once on the walkway, in a state of considerable confusion, she automatically took the turnings and changes that brought her home, to the apartment she shared with her ruined friend, Dolores.

"Oh, my sainted mother," Dolores squealed when Beatrice came in, "will you just look at *this!" This* was a dress that Dolores held out, fresh from its tissue wrappings, a garment of artistic cut and impeccable design that shimmered and reflected the lights with an infinite number of golden mirrors, that in the luxury of its appearance seemed to be spun from real gold. In fact it was real pure eighteen-karat gold, though neither girl knew it.

"It's from *him,"* Beatrice said, as coldly as she could, turning away, though not without an effort, from the seductive garment. Then she explained what had happened, and when she had finished Dolores stroked the dress and smiled, and spoke.

"Then you're going to date him?" she said. "Not for my sake, of course—what's fifty thousand, I mean—you know. Go out for your own sake—enjoy, enjoy."

Beatrice gave a little gasp. "Do you mean—you want me to go out with *him!* After what he did to you?"

"Well it's done, and maybe we should at least profit

from it. And I'll go halfies with you on the loot. And you'll get a meal out of it. But just take my advice, stay out of that back seat of his car."

"You never told me the details . . ."

"Don't sound so stuffy; it's not so sordid as that—I mean, not like in the grubby back of some college kid's car. It was after the theater; I was waiting for a cab when this big car pulls up and he offers to drive me home. What harm? What with a driver and two mugs in the front seat. But who was to know the windows get dark, the lights fade, the whole back of the car turns into a bed with silk sheets, soft music, drinks. To be truthful, honey, it happened so sudden and unreal, like in a dream, I didn't even know it was happening until it was over and I was getting out of the car. At least you'll get a meal. All I got was a run in my stocking plus I saved the cab fare."

Beatrice thought about this, then looked shocked. "You are not suggesting for a moment that—you know what—will happen to me, too? I'm not that kind of girl."

"Neither was I, but I never stood a chance."

"I do." Spoken firmly, with her sweet jaw pushed forward stubbornly, and the light of righteous wrath in her gray-green eyes. "No man can force me to . . . do anything against my will."

"You show 'em, honey," Dolores said, caressing the dress. "And enjoy your dinner."

At six a liveried footman brought perfume—Arpège, and in a pint bottle, too.

At six thirty another liveried footman brought a mutation smoke-gray mink stole and a note, which read, "To keep your precious shoulders warm." The golden dress was sleeveless and strapless, and the stole did go with it, and the effect in the mirror was stunning and at seven, when the door annunciator hummed again, she was ready and she left, head high and proud. She would show him.

The liveried footman who escorted her out said, "Mr. Lowell-Stein has sent his personal copter instead of his car and has said . . ." He touched a button on his jacket and Ron's melodious voice spoke, saying, "The hastier the transport, the sooner you will be with me, my darling."

"Lead the way," she said sharply, though secretly she was glad not to be traveling in his automotive bedroom—though of course the copter might hold its secrets as well.

If it did, it did not reveal them. Instead it took her swiftly and surely to a marble balcony high on the glossy flank of Lowell-Stein House: that remarkable structure, office building and home, that was the seat of power of the Lowell-Stein World Industries. He handed her down himself.

"You are lovely, charming, welcome to my home," he said, tanned, handsome, and respectable, the perfect host, and Beatrice decided on the bold course, hoping to gain the emotional upper hand.

"This is a very nice copter," she said, as coldly as she could, "and at least it doesn't turn into a flying bagnio at the touch of a button."

"But it does, though that is not for you. For you, dinner and the theater first."

"How dare you!"

"I dare nothing. You dare by coming here; you told me that. Now step inside"— the glass wall rose as they approached then sank behind them— "and have a cocktail. I am old-fashioned and we shall have a traditional drink. A martini. Vodka or gin—which do you prefer?"

Ron pointed to Goya's "Maja Desnuda," the original, of course, which whisked from sight disclosing a window behind which moved, in an apparently endless stream, bottle after bottle of every brand of vodka and gin ever manufactured since the world was young. Beatrice concealed her ignorance, quite well she thought, not only of the preferred brand but of the very nature of *martini* itself, by waving gently and saying, "You're the host, why don't you choose for both of us?"

"Capital. We shall have Bombay gin and essence of Noilly Prat, at a thousand to one—the way it should be served."

The automated bar heard him and the bottles whizzed by the window and stopped and Queen Victoria frowned down upon them. The glass fell away and a chromed arm plucked out the bottle, opened it, tilted it, and poured its contents into the air.

"Oh," Beatrice gasped as the liquid fell toward the rug in a transparent stream.

"A bit showy," he said, "but I like things that are done with style," as, at the last instant, a goblet appeared from a hidden niche and caught the drink, every drop.

It was charming to watch, a functional mobile that entertained with its sprightly motions in operation and concluded by producing the desired drink. The silver band on the goblet was caught by a magnetic field and lifted to eye level, floating freely in the air before them. A chime sounded and an atomizer of vermouth essence sprang out on the end of a cunningly jointed arm and poised itself above the container. Ron reached out a casual finger and touched the bulb, which sent a delicate spray across the surface of the gin.

"I like the personal touch," he said. "I feel that it makes the drink."

Then—one, two, three—a cryogenic tube of liquid helium dipped and spun and lifted away, chilling the drink exactly to within a thousandth of the required degree, and a tray, with two glasses cooled to the same temperature as the liquid, appeared on the end of a telescoping gilded arm to the accompaniment of another chime and Ron asked, "Onion or lemon peel?"

"Whichever you suggest," she laughed, enchanted by the device.

"Both," he smiled. "Let us be sybarites tonight." A tube delivered the onions, forked fingers the slips of lemon, and he handed her her glass.

"A toast," he said, "to our love."

"Don't be rude," she told him, sipping. "I think this is quite good."

"To know it is to love it. I was not rude; I was just reminding you that before the night is gone you will have enjoyed ecstasy."

"Nothing of the sort." She put the drink down, and her foot as well. "I am hungry and I wish to go out and eat."

"Forgive me for not telling you, but we are dining at home. I know you will enjoy the meal, it's *ristaffel*, your favorite, since I know how wild you are about Indonesian food." As he spoke he touched her elbow and led her toward the dining room. "We shall begin with *loempia*, then on to *nasi-goreng sambal olek,* and for the wine—the wine!—I have discovered the perfect wine to accompany this exotic meal."

Music swelled as the *gamelan* orchestra began to play, and the temple dancers glided forth. The table was already set and the first course served and steaming, the tiers of cups of spices and sauces rotating slowly, and Beatrice knew that the rice would be perfect and fluffy. She did love this food, but he took too much for granted. She would be firm, even embarrass him.

"I used to like this," she said, trying to look bored while saliva rose to the delightful odors, "but no more. What I prefer is . . ." What? She tried to think of something exotic. "I really prefer . . . Danish food, those delightful open sandwiches."

"To think of the terrible mistake I almost made," Ron said. "Remove this meal."

Beatrice recoiled as the floor opened and the food, dishes, table—even the chairs, dropped through the opening and, an instant before the floor closed again, she heard the beginning of a terrible crash. Good God, he had thrown it all away, silverware, crystal, the lot. The orchestra and dancers were whisked away by their podium and for a dreadful moment she was afraid *they* were bound for the incinerator too.

"Do you like Rembrandt?" he asked, pointing to an immense painting that covered the rear wall. She turned to look. 'The Night Watch,' one of my favorites."

"I thought it was in Holland . . ." she began, then turned her head at a sound behind her and could not finish.

A long, oaken table with two matching refectory chairs had appeared and was laden with tier upon tier of food.

"Smorrebrod," Ron said, "to be correct, since they are not really sandwiches. There are five hundred here, so I'm sure you will find your favorites. And beer, Tuborg F.F., of course; really this is the only fine food that is to be eaten with beer, and *akvavit,* the sly Danish *snaps,* served frozen in a block of ice. There are rules, you know."

She had not known, but she was learning. She served herself and ate, and her thoughts flickered like the candles before her, and before she was through she was stern and firm again, because she knew what was happening.

"You think you can buy me with your money," she told him, as she spooned up the last mouthful of *rodegrod med flode.* "I am supposed to be impressed, grateful for all this, so grateful that I will let you do . . . what you want to do."

"Not at all." He smiled, and his smile was sincerely charming. "I will not deny that there are girls that can be bought with trinkets and meals, but not you. All this, as you so charmingly put it, is here merely for our pleasure while I am determining what your excuse will be."

"I don't understand."

"You will. In simpler cultures lovers clasp to one another in mutual agreement, no aggressor, no loser. We have lost this simplicity and substituted for it a ritualized game. It is called seduction. Women are seduced by men, therefore remain pure. When in reality they have both enjoyed the union of love, mankind's greatest glory and pleasure, and the word *seduction* is just the excuse the women use to permit it. Every woman has some hidden excuse that she calls seduction, and the artifice of man is in finding that excuse."

"Not I!"

"Yes, you. Yours is not one of the common ones. You will not seek the simple excuse of excessive drink, rough force, simple gratitude, or anything so plebeian. But we shall find it; before dawn we will know."

"I'll hear no more," she said, dropping her spoon and standing. "I wish to leave for the theater now." Once out of this place she knew she would be safe; she would not return.

"By all means, permit me," he held out his arm and she took it. They walked toward the far wall, which lifted silently to reveal a theater within which there were just two seats. "I have hired the entire Yugoslavian company for the evening; they are waiting to begin."

Speechless she sat, and by the end of the performance her mind was still as unsettled as when she had come in. As they applauded she waited, tensely, for him to make his move, so tightly wound that she started visibly when he took her hand.

"You must not," he said, "be afraid of me or of violence. That is not for you, my darling. For you, for us, now there is a glass of simple cognac while we discuss the delightful Serbo-Croatian performance that we have just seen."

They exited through the only door, which led now to a brocaded room where a Hungarian violinist played gypsy airs. As they seated themselves at the table a tailcoated waiter appeared carrying a bottle on a plush cushion. He placed it, with immense care, upon the center of the table, then withdrew.

"I trust no one but myself to open a bottle like this; the corks are fragile as dust," Ron said, then added, "I imagine that you have never tasted Napoleon brandy before?"

"If it's from California I have," she told him, with all sincerity. He closed his eyes.

"No," he said, in a slightly choked voice, "it is not from the State of California, but France, the land of the mother of wines. Distilled, bottled and laid gently down during the brief but glorious reign of the Emperor Napoleon Bonaparte . . ."

"But that must be hundreds and hundreds of years ago?"

"Exactly. Each year this emperor of cognacs grows a little—and grows more scarce. I have men working for me whose only occupation is to scour the world for more, to pay any price. I will not profane a conversation about beauty by mentioning what was paid for this one. You must judge for yourself if it was worth it."

As he talked he had been working, delicately and skillfully, to extract the cork, undamaged, and it slid free and he placed it on a napkin. Into each round-bellied snifter he poured but a golden half inch and gave one to her.

"Breathe in the bouquet first, before you take the smallest sip," he told her, and she obeyed.

A hush fell on the room as they touched the glasses to their lips and she raised her face in awe, tears in eyes, saying, "Why . . . . it's, it's . . ."

"I know," he said with a whisper and as he leaned forward the dim lights darkened even more and the fiddler slipped from sight. His lips brushed the white, bare flesh of her shoulder, kissed it, then moved to her throat.

"Ohh," she gasped, and raised her hand to caress his head. "No!" she said even louder, and pulled away.

"Very close," he smiled, leaning back in his chair. "Very close indeed. You are a creature of ardent passions; we have but to find the key."

"Never," she said firmly, and he laughed.

As they finished their brandy the lights grew brighter and, unnoticed, a silvery blade flashed from the leg of her chair, nicked the hem of her skirt, then vanished. Ron took her hand, and when she rose the dress began to unravel and a rain of golden particles fell to the floor.

"My dress," she said, and clutched at the disintegrating edge. "What's happening to it?"

"It is going," he said, then seated himself again so he could look on in comfort.

Faster and faster the process went and she could not stop it until, within moments, the dress was gone and, like heaped bullion, a golden mound rested about her feet.

"Black lace against white flesh," he said, smiling approval. "You did that just for me. With sweet pink ribbons for your stockings."

"This is crude and rude of you and I hate you. Give me back my clothes," she said fiercely, fists clenched at her sides, too proud to attempt to cover her wispy undergarments with her hands.

"Bravo. You are a redhead of temperament and I have to admire you. Through that door you will find a dressing room and bathing costume, for we shall swim."

"I don't want . . ." she said, but to no avail for the floor moved and carried her through the door into a discreet and elegant boudoir where a black-and-white-garbed French maid was waiting. The maid had an elegantly simple, one-piece, white bathing suit on her arm and she smiled as padded arms gripped Beatrice and flashing devices stripped her remaining clothes from her in an instant.

"Do not fret zee pretty head, mademoiselle," the maid said, holding out the suit. "They were of no value and zee replacements you shall treasure for years. If you please."

"I've been rushed, but I have no choice. None of this will do him any good," Beatrice said, then tried to pull away as sudden clamps seized her again and something small and cold and solid was inserted into each of her delicate nostrils.

"How wonderful is the modern science," the maid said as she patted away the last wrinkle on the skintight suit, which fitted to perfection. "Remember to breathe only through your nose and it will be like fresh breezes. *Au revoir et bonne chance.*"

Before Beatrice could protest or her raised hand could touch her nose the floor opened and she fell through into the water. She kept her mouth closed and sank under its luminescent surface and found she could breathe as easily as she had always done, and the sensation was wonderful, or novel to say the least. There was music, carried to her ears clearly by the conducting water, and white sand below, and she dived and turned and would have laughed aloud, if she were able, her riotous red hair streaming behind her.

Ron swam up, handsome and tanned in a pair of white trunks to match her suit, and smiled charmingly, then twisted under and tickled her foot. She turned, smiling too, and darted away, but he followed and they did a breathless dance of three dimensions through the crystal water, around and about, free, unhampered, happy.

Deliciously tired she floated, suspended, her eyes closed, and felt his arms against her back and the entire strong length of his body against hers and his lips on hers and hers answering . . .

"*No* . . ." she said aloud and a great bubble arose from her mouth. Her fingers tore at her nostrils and there was a sudden, brief pain as the devices were pulled free and fell, twinkling down from her hand. "I would rather die first," she said with the last of her air.

With a gurgling *woosh* the pool emptied and they sat on the damp sand below. "Woman of will," Ron said, handing her an acre-sized white towel, "I do love you. Now we shall dance, a gavotte; you will enjoy that. There is a string quartet and we will wear the costume of the proper time, you gorgeous in high white wig and low, wide décolletage . . ."

"No. I'm going home." She shivered and wrapped the towel tighter about her body.

"Of course, dancing would be too commonplace for you. Instead we will . . ."

"No. My clothes. I'm going. You cannot stop me."

He bowed, graceful as always, and gestured her toward a door that had opened in the wall. "Dress yourself; I said violence was not for you. Violence is not your excuse."

"I h-have no excuse," she said through chattering teeth, and wondered why she shivered since she was so warm.

The little maid was waiting and stripped her down and dried her while a miraculous machine did her hair in seconds, though, in all truth, Beatrice was not aware of this, or even aware of being unaware, as her thoughts darted and spun like maddened butterflies. Only when the maid offered her a dress did she order her thoughts, push it away, push aside the closets of awe-inspiring garments, all her size, to find a simple black suit buried in the back. It had a curve-hugging and breathless simplicity, but it was the best she could do. Powdered, manicured, made up, she had no awareness of it or of the passing of time until, born anew, she stood before him in a chaste and oak-paneled room.

"A last drink," he said, nodding at the Napoleon brandy on the table.

"I'm going," she shouted, because for some reason she wanted to stay. Hurling herself past him she tore open the door on the far wall and slammed it behind her. A stairway stretched up and down and she ran down it, flight after flight, gasping for breath, until she could run no more. For a moment she rested against the wall, then straightened and touched her hair, opened the door and stepped through into the same room she had left high above.

"A last drink," he said, lifting the bottle.

Speechless this time, she ran, closed the door, climbed upwards, higher, until her strength was gone and the stairs ended with a dusty fire door leading to the roof. Opening it she threw herself through into the same room she had left far below.

"A last drink," he said, decanting the golden drops, then glancing up to notice how her eyes flew to the other doors around the room. "All doors, all halls, all stairs, lead back here," he said, not unkindly. "You must have this drink. Sit. Rest. Drink. A toast. To love, my darling."

Exhausted, she held the glass in both hands, warming it with the heat of her body, then drank. It was heavenly and his face was close beside hers and his lips were whispering in her ear.

"Would you believe," the hushed sibilants sounded, "would you believe that this brandy contains a drug that destroys your will to say no? Resistance is useless, you are mine."

No, no . . . her lips said, while her arms said yes, yes, and pulled her to him. No, no, never, never, and darkness descended.

"Drugs, mind-destroying drugs," she said later, in the warm darkness, their fingertips just touching, cool sheets against her back, her voice a little smug and satisfied. "There was no other way, drugs against my will."

"Do you believe," his shocked voice answered, "that I would put anything at all in *that* brandy? Of course not, my darling. We have just found your excuse, that is all."

A CIVIL SERVICE SERVANT

Precisely at nine in the morning the post office opened and the first customers were allowed to enter. Howards knew this, yet, as he straightened his Book on the counter before him, he could not prevent himself from glancing worriedly at the big clock on the wall. Why? This was just a work day like any other day. God, the fear, deep down, as the long black pointer clicked another notch toward the vertical.

Just another day, why should he be so concerned? He tittered nervously and turned his key in the lock of the multifrank before him, just as two people appeared on the other side of the counter.

"I wish to post this letter to Sierra Leone," the man said.

"A two-credit insurance stamp," the woman said.

Instantly, they began to squabble as to which of them had been there first, their voices crescendoing shriller and higher. Howards slapped his left hand on the Book and raised his right.

"Stop," he said, and they did, struck by the authority in his voice. "Reference B-86Y/234 in the Book of Postal Regulations states that all differences of opinion and priority are to be settled by the serving clerk. That is myself. Ladies first. Here is your insurance stamp, madam."

His fingers were snapping over the complex controls of the multifrank even as he spoke, and he was secretly proud of the assured way that he said it. The man stepped aside, the woman timidly proffered her insurance book as he stood with his finger poised over the activate button. With his free hand he flipped the book open, dropped it into the slot and pressed the button.

"That will be twenty-two credits eighty, madam." The bills went into the cash receptacle and her change rattled into the delivery cup. "Next," he said, not without a certain amount of condescension.

The man said nothing; he knew better than to argue. He certainly did. What was in the Book was correct. The man stepped away and Howards thought that this day had certainly begun busily enough: but why the little shivering knot of fear, Howards? he wondered to himself, and rubbed at the spot in his midriff with his knuckles.

A large, dark man with a full black beard filled the space outside the counter. "Do you know what this is?" he bellowed.

"I certainly do," Howards said. (Did his voice crack a little?) "That is a needle gun."

"You are correct," the man hissed in a voice like the breaking of poison waves. "It fires a needle soundlessly with such great speed that contact with the human body produces a hydrostatic wave that utterly destroys the nervous system. Would you like that?" White teeth appeared in the tangle of black beard.

"I would not like my nervous system utterly destroyed."

"You will then pay me the sum of four thousand, nine hundred and ninety-nine credits."

"I have no till or money. Cash is centrally supplied . . ."

"Fool! I know all that. I also know that the payment of any sum over five thousand credits must be especially authorized for any position. Therefore—four thousand nine hundred ninety-nine credits. At once."

"At once," Howards said crisply, and spoke aloud as he hit the keys. "Four, nine, nine, nine . . ."

"Now activate."

Howards hesitated for a mere fraction of an instant, sucked in his breath, then snapped his finger down on the activate button.

There was the rattle of small change from the delivery cup and the man glanced down at it just as a gush of white vapor shot out into his face. He screamed and writhed and fell as the full force of the regurgitants, irritants, and vesicants hit him at once.

"Foolish man," Howards said into the handkerchief he

raised to his face, stepping back, away from the gas. "Security was onto him as soon as I rang up four hundred and ninety-nine million, nine hundred thousand credits. Just a simple decimal shift . . ."

It was almost nine and the first customer would be in soon. A day like any other day—then why was he feeling this way? What way? As if he were imprisoned in the back of his own brain and screaming. Foolishness, this was not a proper thought for a public servant to have.

"Help me," the old woman said just as the black hand touched the hour.

"Of course, madam." Where had she come from, like that, so quickly?

"It is my pension," pushing a battered and torn payment book across the counter with her scaling, shivering hand. "They will not pay me my money."

"Money due is always paid," Howards said, flipping open the rusty book while trying to touch it only with the tips of his fingers. He pointed to a torn fragment of paper. "Here is the reason. The page is missing. To authorize payment you must get form 925/1k(43) and have it filled out."

"I have it," the woman told him, and pushed over—almost threw, in fact—an even more creased and soiled piece of paper. Howards hoped that none of his feelings were revealed on his face as he turned and read it.

"This is the correct form, madam, but it is not completely filled out. In this blank here you must enter your deceased husband's insurance number."

"I do not know his number," the woman shrilled and clutched tightly to the counter's edge. "He is dead and his papers, they were all destroyed, you see."

"In that case you must obtain form 276/po(67), which is an application to the proper authorities for the required information." He pushed the papers with what he hoped was a smile. "You can obtain an application for this form . . ."

"I will die first," the old woman screamed and threw all her papers into the air so that they fluttered down around her like filthy confetti. "I have not eaten for a week. I demand justice. I must have money for food . . ."

It was all quite distasteful. "I wish I could oblige,

madam, but I have no authority. You should apply for the form of application to see the Emergency officer . . ."

"I will be dead first!" she shouted hoarsely, and thrust her face toward his. He could smell her sour breath and quickly withdrew. "Have you no pity on someone my age? I could be your mother."

"Thankfully, madam, you are not. My mother has the proper forms . . ."

"Forms!" Her voice screeched higher and higher until it cracked. "You care more for forms than for human life. I swore I would kill myself unless I obtained money for food today. Save me!"

"Please do not threaten. I have done what I can." Had he? Was there some authority he should summon? Was he correct . . .

"Better a quick death than one of slow starvation. Money—or I die!"

She had a large bread knife now and was waving it before him. Was this a threat? Did it call for the guards?

"I cannot . . ." Howards gasped, and his fingers hovered over the keys in an agony of indecision. Guards? Doctor? Police?

"Then I die, and it is a world I do not regret losing."

She held one hand on the counter, palm up, and with a savage slash of the knife almost severed the hand from the wrist. Thick blood spurted high.

"What have you done?" he shouted and reached for the keys. But she began to scream and wave her arm and blood spattered him and gushed over the counter.

"The Book!" he gasped. "You're getting blood on the Book. You cannot." He pulled it away and began to dab at it with his handkerchief, then remembered that he had not yet summoned help. He hesitated, torn, then put the Book in the farthest corner and rushed back to his position. There was blood everywhere—had he made a mistake?—and the woman had sunk from sight but he could still hear her moans.

"Medical assistance," he said quickly into the microphone. "First aid needed. At once."

Should he do something for her? But he could not leave his station. And the blood, everywhere, on his hands and shirt. He held them out in horror. He had never seen so much blood, human blood, before . . .

And at nine o'clock, precisely, the post office would open. Another day, just like any other.

What was wrong with his hands? Was there something he should remember? Like a vanishing echo a memory rushed away—a memory of what? There was nothing wrong: he was at his position where he belonged, with his Book close at hand and the shining mass of the multifrank before him. He belonged, of course he belonged—then why, again, a fleeting, fading, frightening memory that it was wrong?

Why was he looking at his hands?

Howards shivered and unlocked the machine and cleared it, flipped the test and operational switch so the light glowed green, checked the cleared reading and set up 4,999 . . .

This was not right. Why had he done it? With a furtive glance over his shoulder he quickly cleared the machine. The long black hand of the clock clicked one notch forward and was vertical and an immense queue of people formed outside his position. They were jammed solid, all looking at him, quiet now, though there was a murmur from the rear.

"Good morning, sir," he said to the red-faced gentleman who headed the line. "What may I . . ."

"None of your conversation. I want service not chatter. This letter, special delivery, at once, to Capitello, Salerno, Italy. What will it cost?"

"That depends," Howards said, reaching for the envelope, which the man pulled back.

"Depends upon what, damn it? I want to mail this thing, not talk about it."

There was a murmur of impatience from the waiting people and, smiling insincerely, Howards said, "It depends upon the weight, sir. Special delivery letters are delivered by orbiting rocket and the charge varies according to the weight."

"Then you can damn well stop talking about it and weigh it," he said, thrusting the letter forward.

Howards took it, dropped it into the slot, then read off the price.

"Too damn much," the man shouted. "Mailed a letter

to Capitello yesterday and it cost less."

"It probably weighed less, sir."

"I wanna mail this package," a small child said, thrusting an untidy bundle onto the counter.

"Are you calling me a liar?" the red-face man shouted, growing even redder.

"No, sir—just a minute, sonny—I simply stated that if it cost less it weighed less . . ."

"Damn nerve, call a man a liar, ought to thrash you. Wish to see your supervisor at once."

"My supervisor does not see the public. If you wish to file a complaint the Complaint Office is in Room eight nine three four—don't do that!" he added as the child pushed the package further across the counter so that it slid off the inner edge and fell to the floor. Something inside broke with a loud plop and an awful stench seeped out.

"You broke it!" the child screamed.

"I did not; take it at once," Howards said, picking it up by an end of string and dangling it outside. The child ignored it and began to cry loudly.

"Man ought to be horsewhipped, treating a child like that!"

"Room eight nine three four," Howards said through clenched lips, hoping the man would leave.

A tall young man with red hair was bobbing up and down behind the weeping child. "I would like to send a telegram to my uncle saying 'Dear Uncle, Need at Once Credits One Hundred . . .' "

"Would you please fill out the telegraph form," Howards said, pressing the switch that delivered a printed form into the dispenser outside.

"Bit of difficulty," the young man said, holding up both of his hands, which were swathed in bandages and plaster. "Can't write, but I can dictate it to you, won't take a moment. 'Dear Uncle . . .' "

"I am very sorry but I cannot accept dictated telegrams. However any public phone will take them."

"Bit of trouble getting the coins in the slot. 'Dear Uncle . . . ?' "

"Cruel and heartless," the young girl next in line sniffed.

"I would like to help you," Howards said, "but it is forbidden by regulations. However I am sure that someone near the end of the line will write your telegram for you, then I will be happy to accept it."

"How very smart of you," the young girl said. She was exceedingly attractive and when she leaned forward her breasts rested tidily on the counter's edge. She smiled. "I would like to buy some stamps," she said.

Howards smiled back, with utmost sincerity this time. "I would be extremely happy to oblige, miss, except for the fact that we no longer issue stamps. The amount of postage is printed directly on the envelope."

"How clever of you. But isn't it possible to buy commemorative stamps still held in the postal vaults?"

"Of course, that is a different matter. Sale to the public of commemorative issues is authorized in the Book by Reference Y-23H/48."

"How very intelligent of you to remember all of that! Then I would like the Centenary of the Automatic Diaper Service . . ."

"Nerve, damned nerve, trying to get rid of me," the red face said, thrusting across at him. "Room eight nine four four is closed."

"I have no doubt that Room eight nine four four is closed," Howards said calmly. "I do not know what is in Room eight nine four four. But the Complaints Office is in Room eight nine three four."

"Then why in blazes did you tell me eight nine four four?"

"I did not."

"You did!"

"Never. I do not make that kind of mistake."

Mistake? Howards thought. Mistake! Oh, no.

"I'm afraid I have made a small mistake," he said, white-faced, to the girl. "There is a later special order on the entry canceling the issue of all commemorative stamps across the counter."

"But that should make no difference," she said, pouting prettily. "You can sell me a little teensy diaper stamp . . ."

"If it was within my power nothing would give me greater pleasure, but the regulations cannot be broken."

"Your head can be broken just like you broke this!" an

immense and angry man said, thrusting the girl aside and pushing the crumbled package under Howards's nose. The stench was overwhelming.

"I assure you, sir, I did not break that. Would you kindly remove . . ."

"My son said you did."

"Nevertheless, I did not."

"Call my boy a liar!" the man roared and reached across the counter and grabbed Howards by the shirt.

"Stop that," Howards gasped and tried to pull away and heard the material tear. He groped out and hit the guard switch. It snapped off clean and rattled to the floor. Howards pulled back harder and most of his shirt came away in the man's hand.

"Stamp, please," someone said and a letter dropped into the slot.

"That will be two credits," Howards said, hitting the breakdown button then ringing up the postage.

"You said Room eight nine four four," the red face shouted.

"Been mistreating the machine," a sour-faced repairman said, appearing beside Howards.

"Never, I just touched it and it broke."

"These machines never break."

"Help me," a frail old woman said, pushing a battered and torn payment book across the counter with a scaly and shaking hand. "It is my pension. They will not pay me my money."

"Money due is always paid," Howards said, closing his eyes for an instant—why?—then reaching for the book. He caught sight of the man pushing up to the counter, a man with a tangle of black beard and a hateful expression.

"I know . . ." Howards began, then stopped. What did he know? Something pressed hard inside his head and tried to burst out.

"I do not know his number," the old woman screamed. "He is dead and his papers, they were all destroyed, you see."

"Do you know what this is? It is a needle gun."

"Not in Room eight nine four four."

"Just one diaper . . ."

Howards clutched graspingly at his head and did not

know if he was screaming or if he was hearing someone else scream.

Welcome blackness engulfed him.

"Now just sip this and you will find yourself feeling fine in a few moments."

Howards took the cup that the Examiner held out to him and was surprised to discover that he needed both hands to hold it. He noticed that the backs of his hands were beaded with sweat. As he sipped he felt the helmet lifting from his head and when he looked up he had a swift glimpse of it just before it vanished through a recess in the ceiling.

"The examination—aren't you going to proceed?"

The Examiner chuckled and steepled his heavy fingers on the desk before him. "A not uncommon reaction," he said. "The examination is complete."

"I have no memory. It seemed as though the helmet came down, then went up again. Though my hands are covered with sweat." He looked at them, then shivered with realization. "Then the examination is over. And I . . ."

"You must have patience," the Examiner told him with ponderous dignity. "The results must be analyzed, compared, a report drawn up. Even electronically this takes time. You should not complain."

"Oh, I am not complaining, Examiner," Howards said quickly, lowering his eyes. "I am grateful."

"You should be. Just think of the way all of this used to be. Hours of oral and written examinations, with the best marks going to the crammers. You can't cram for a simulator examination."

"I do know that, Examiner."

"Just a few moments of unconsciousness and the machine mentally puts you through your paces, puts you into situations and judges how you respond to them. Real situations that a postal clerk would face during the normal course of his duties."

"Normal duties, of course," Howards said, frowning at his hands, then wiping them quickly against his side.

The Examiner stared at the figures that raced across the screen on his desk. "Not as good as I expected,

Howards," he said sternly. "You'll not be a postal clerk this year."

"But—I was so sure—the twelfth time."

"There is more to clerking than just knowing the Book. Go away. Study. Apply yourself. Your grade this time is high enough so that your student's status will continue for another year. Work harder. Very few students are carried past their fifteenth year."

Howards stood, helplessly, and turned before he left.

"My wife asked me, to ask you, we're not getting younger. Planning permission for a child . . ."

"Out of the question. There is the population problem for one thing, and your status for another. If you were a clerk the application might be considered."

"But there are so few clerks," Howards said weakly.

"There are so few positions. Be happy you are a registered student with rations and quarters. Do you know what it is like to be an Under-unemployed?"

"Thank you, sir. Good-bye, sir. You have been most kind."

Howards closed the door quickly behind him—why did he keep thinking there was blood on his hands? He shook his head to clear it.

It would be hard to tell Dora. She had hoped so.

But at least he still had his Book. And a whole year to memorize it again. That would be good. And there would be inserts and additions, that was always good.

He walked by the post office in the lobby of the building with his eyes averted.

A CRIMINAL ACT

The first blow of the hammer shook the door in its frame, and the second blow made the thin wood boom like a drum. Benedict Vernall threw the door open before a third stroke could fall and pushed his gun into the stomach of the man with the hammer.

"Get going. Get out of here," Benedict said, in a much shriller voice than he had planned to use.

"Don't be foolish," the bailiff said quietly, stepping aside so that the two guards behind him in the hall were clearly visible. "I am the bailiff and I am doing my duty. If I am attacked these men have orders to shoot you and everyone else in your apartment. Be intelligent. Yours is not the first case like this. Such things are planned for."

One of the guards clicked off the safety catch on his submachine gun, smirking at Benedict as he did it. Benedict let the pistol fall slowly to his side.

"Much better," the bailiff told him and struck the nail once more with the hammer so that the notice was fixed firmly to the door.

"Take that filthy thing down," Benedict said, choking over the words.

"Benedict Vernall," the bailiff said, adjusting his glasses on his nose as he read from the proclamation he had just posted. "This is to inform you that pursuant to the Criminal Birth Act of 1993 you are guilty of the act of criminal birth and are hereby proscribed and no longer protected from bodily injury by the forces of this sovereign state . . ."

"You're going to let some madman kill me—what kind of a dirty law is that?"

The bailiff removed his glasses and gazed coldly along

his nose at Benedict. "Mr. Vernall," he said, "have the decency to accept the results of your own actions. Did you or did you not have an illegal baby?"

"Illegal—never! A harmless infant . . ."

"Do you or do you not already have the legal maximum of two children?"

"We have two, but . . ."

"You refused advice or aid from your local birth-control clinic. You expelled, with force, the birth guidance officer who called upon you. You rejected the offer of the abortion clinic . . ."

"Murderers!"

". . . and the advice of the Family Planning Board. The statutory six months have elapsed without any action on your part. You have had the three advance warnings and have ignored them. Your family still contains one consumer more than is prescribed by law, therefore the proclamation has been posted. You alone are responsible, Mr. Vernall, you can blame no one else."

"I can blame this foul law."

"It is the law of the land," the bailiff said, drawing himself up sternly. "It is not for you or me to question." He took a whistle from his pocket and raised it to his mouth. "It is my legal duty to remind you that you still have one course open, even at this last moment, and may still avail yourself of the services of the Euthanasia Clinic."

"Go straight to hell!"

"Indeed. I've been told that before." The bailiff snapped the whistle to his lips and blew a shrill blast. He almost smiled as Benedict slammed shut the apartment door.

There was an animal-throated roar from the stairwell as the policemen who were blocking it stepped aside. A knot of fiercely tangled men burst out, running and fighting at the same time. One of them surged ahead of the pack but fell as a fist caught him on the side of the head; the others trampled him underfoot. Shouting and cursing the mob came on and it looked as though it would be a draw, but a few yards short of the door one of the leaders tripped and brought two others down. A short fat man in the second rank leaped their bodies and crashed headlong into Vernall's door with such force that the ballpoint pen he held extended pierced the paper of the notice and sank into the wood beneath.

"A volunteer has been selected," the bailiff shouted and the waiting police and guards closed in on the wailing men and began to force them back toward the stairs. One of the men remained behind on the floor, saliva running down his cheeks as he chewed hysterically at a strip of the threadbare carpet. Two white-garbed hospital attendants were looking out for this sort of thing and one of them jabbed the man expertly in the neck with a hypodermic needle while the other unrolled the stretcher.

Under the bailiff's watchful eye the volunteer painstakingly wrote his name in the correct space on the proclamation, then carefully put the pen back in his vest pocket.

"Very glad to accept you as a volunteer for this important public duty, Mr. . . ." the bailiff leaned forward to peer at the paper, "Mr. Mortimer," he said.

"Mortimer is my first name," the man said in a crisply dry voice as he dabbed lightly at his forehead with his breast-pocket handkerchief.

"Understandable, sir, your anonymity will be respected as is the right of all volunteers. Might I presume that you are acquainted with the rest of the regulations?"

"You may. Paragraph forty-six of the Criminal Birth Act of 1993, subsection fourteen, governing the selection of volunteers. Firstly, I have volunteered for the maximum period of twenty-four hours. Secondly, I will neither attempt nor commit violence of any form upon any other members of the public during this time, and if I do so I will be held responsible by law for all of my acts."

"Very good. But isn't there more?"

Mortimer folded the handkerchief precisely and tucked it back into his pocket. "Thirdly," he said, and patted it smooth, "I shall not be liable to prosecution by law if I take the life of the proscribed individual, one Benedict Vernall."

"Perfectly correct." The bailiff nodded and pointed to a large suitcase that a policeman had set down on the floor and was opening. The hall had been cleared. "If you would step over here and take your choice." They both gazed down into the suitcase that was filled to overflowing with instruments of death. "I hope you also understand that your own life will be in jeopardy during this period and if you are injured or killed you will not be protected by law?"

"Don't take me for a fool," Mortimer said curtly, then pointed into the suitcase. "I want one of those concussion grenades."

"You cannot have it," the bailiff told him in a cutting voice, injured by the other's manner. There was a correct way to do these things. "Those are only for use in open districts where the innocent cannot be injured. Not in an apartment building. You have your choice of all the short-range weapons, however."

Mortimer laced his fingers together and stood with his head bowed, almost in an attitude of prayer, as he examined the contents. Machine pistols, grenades, automatics, knives, knuckle dusters, vials of acid, whips, straight razors, broken glass, poison darts, morning stars, maces, gas bombs, and tear-gas pens.

"Is there any limit?" he asked.

"Take what you feel you will need. Just remember that it must all be accounted for and returned."

"I want the Reisling machine pistol with five of the twenty-cartridge magazines and the commando knife with the spikes on the handguard and fountain-pen tear-gas gun."

The bailiff was making quick check marks on a mimeographed form attached to his clip board while Mortimer spoke. "Is that all?" he asked.

Mortimer nodded and took the extended board and scrawled his name on the bottom of the sheet without examining it, then began at once to fill his pockets with the weapons and ammunition.

"Twenty-four hours," the bailiff said, looking at his watch and filling in one more space in the form. "You have until 1745 hours tomorrow."

"Get away from the door, please, Ben," Maria begged.

"Quiet," Benedict whispered, his ear pressed to the panel. "I want to hear what they are saying." His face screwed up as he struggled to understand the muffled voices. "It's no good," he said, turning away. "I can't make it out. Not that it makes any difference. I know what's happening . . ."

"There's a man coming to kill you," Maria said in her delicate, little girl's voice. The baby started to whimper and she hugged him to her.

"Please, Maria, go back into the bathroom like we agreed. You have the bed in there, and the food, and there aren't any windows. As long as you stay along the wall away from the door nothing can possibly happen to you. Do that for me, darling—so I won't have to worry about either of you."

"Then you will be out here alone."

Benedict squared his narrow shoulders and clutched the pistol firmly. "That is where I belong, out in front, defending my family. That is as old as the history of man."

"Family," she said and looked around worriedly. "What about Matthew and Agnes?"

"They'll be all right with your mother. She promised to look after them until we got in touch with her again. You can still be there with them; I wish you would."

"No, I couldn't. I couldn't bear being anywhere else now. And I couldn't leave the baby there; he would be so hungry." She looked down at the infant, who was still whimpering, then began to unbutton the top of her dress.

"Please, darling," Benedict said, edging back from the door. "I want you to go into the bathroom with baby and stay there. You must. He could be coming at any time now."

She reluctantly obeyed him, and he waited until the door had closed and he heard the lock being turned. Then he tried to force their presence from his mind because they were only a distraction that could interfere with what must be done. He had worked out the details of his plan of defense long before and he went slowly around the apartment making sure that everything was as it should be. First the front door, the only door into the apartment. It was locked and bolted and the night chain was attached. All that remained was to push the big wardrobe up against it. The killer could not enter now without a noisy struggle, and if he tried Benedict would be there waiting with his gun. That took care of the door.

There were no windows in either the kitchen or the bathroom, so he could forget about these rooms. The bedroom was a possibility since its window looked out on-to the fire escape, but he had a plan for this too. The window was locked and the only way it could be opened from the outside was by breaking the glass. He would hear that and would have time to push the couch in the hall up against the bedroom door. He didn't want to block it now in case he had to retreat into the bedroom himself.

Only one room remained, the living room, and this was where he was going to make his stand. There were two windows in the living room and the far one could be en-tered from the fire escape, as could the bedroom window. The killer might come this way. The other window could not be reached from the fire escape, though shots could still be fired through it from the windows across the court. But the corner was out of the line of fire, and this was where he would be. He had pushed the big armchair right up against the wall and, after checking once more that both windows were locked, he dropped into it.

His gun rested on his lap and pointed at the far window by the fire escape. He would shoot if anyone tried to come through it. The other window was close by, but no harm could come that way unless he stood in front of it. The thin fabric curtains were drawn and once it was dark he could see through them without being seen himself. By shifting the gun barrel a few degrees he could cover the door into the hall. If there were any disturbance at the front door he could be there in a few steps. He had done everything he could. He settled back into the chair.

Once the daylight faded the room was quite dark, yet he could see well enough by the light of the city sky, which filtered in through the drawn curtains. It was very quiet and whenever he shifted position he could hear the rusty chair springs twang beneath him. After only a few hours he realized one slight flaw in his plan. He was thirsty.

At first he could ignore it, but by nine o'clock his mouth was as dry as cotton wool. He knew he couldn't last the night like this; it was too distracting. He should have brought a jug of water in with him. The wisest thing would be to go and get it as soon as possible, yet he did not want to leave the protection of the corner. He had heard nothing of the killer and this only made him more concerned about his unseen presence.

Then he heard Maria calling to him. Very softly at first, then louder and louder. She was worried. Was he all right? He dared not answer her, not from here. The only thing to do was to go to her, whisper through the door that everything was fine and that she should be quiet. Perhaps then she would go to sleep. And he could get some water in the kitchen and bring it back.

As quietly as he could he rose and stretched his stiff legs, keeping his eyes on the gray square of the second window. Putting the toe of one foot against the heel of the other he pulled his shoes off, then went on silent tiptoe across the room. Maria was calling louder now, rattling at the bathroom door, and he had to silence her. Why couldn't she realize the danger she was putting him in?

As he passed through the door the hall light above him came on.

"What are you doing?" he screamed at Maria who stood by the switch, blinking in the sudden glare.

"I was so worried . . ."

The crash of breaking glass from the living room was punctuated by the hammering boom of the machine pistol. Arrows of pain tore at Benedict and he hurled himself sprawling into the hall.

"Into the bathroom!" he screeched and fired his own revolver back through the dark doorway.

He was only half aware of Maria's muffled squeal as she slammed the door and, for the moment, he forgot the pain of the wounds. There was the metallic smell of burnt gunpowder and a blue haze hung in the air. Something scraped in the living room and he fired again into the darkness. He winced as the answering fire crashed thunder and flame toward him and the bullets tore holes in the plaster of the hall opposite the door.

The firing stopped but he kept his gun pointed as he realized that the killer's fire couldn't reach him where he lay, against the wall away from the open doorway. The man would have to come into the hall to shoot him, and if he did that Benedict would fire first and kill him. More shots slammed into the wall, but he did not bother to answer them. When the silence stretched out for more than a minute he took a chance and silently broke his revolver and pulled out the empty shells, putting live cartridges in their place. There was a pool of blood under his leg.

Keeping the gun pointed at the doorway he clumsily rolled up his pants leg with his left hand, then took a quick glimpse. There was more blood running down his ankle and sopping his sock. A bullet had torn through his calf muscle and made two round, dark holes from which the thick blood pumped. It made him dizzy to look at it, then he remembered and pointed the wavering pistol back at the doorway. The living room was silent. His side hurt too, but when he pulled his shirt out of his trousers and looked he realized that although this wound was painful, it was not as bad as the one in his leg. A second bullet had burned along his side, glancing off the ribs and leaving a shallow wound. It wasn't bleeding badly. Something would have to be done about his leg.

"You moved fast, Benedict, I must congratulate you—"

Benedict's finger contracted with shock and he pumped two bullets into the room, toward the sound of the man's voice. The man laughed.

"Nerves, Benedict, nerves. Just because I am here to kill you doesn't mean that we can't talk."

"You're a filthy beast, a foul, filthy beast!" Benedict splattered the words from his lips and followed them with a string of obscenities, expressions he hadn't used or even heard since his school days. He stopped suddenly as he realized that Maria could hear him. She had never heard him curse before.

"Nerves, Benedict?" The dry laugh sounded again. "Calling me insulting names won't alter this situation."

"Why don't you leave; I won't try to stop you," Benedict said as he slowly pulled his left arm out of his shirt. "I don't want to see you or know you. Why don't you go away?"

"I'm afraid that it is not that easy, Ben. You have created this situation; in one sense you have called me here. Like a sorcerer summoning some evil genie. That's a pleasant simile, isn't it? May I introduce myself. My name is Mortimer."

"I don't want to know your name, you . . . piece of

filth." Benedict half mumbled, his attention concentrated on the silent removal of his shirt. It hung from his right wrist and he shifted the gun to his left hand for a moment while he slipped it off. His leg throbbed with pain when he draped the shirt over the wound in his calf and he gasped, then spoke quickly to disguise the sound. "You came here because you wanted to—and I'm going to kill you for that."

"Very good, Benedict, that is much more the type of spirit I expected from you. After all, you are the closest we can come to a dedicated law-breaker these days, the antisocial individualist who stands alone, who will carry on the traditions of the Dillingers and the James brothers. Though they brought death and you brought life, and your weapon is far humbler than their guns . . ." The words ended with a dry chuckle.

"You have a warped mind, Mortimer, just what I would suspect of a man who accepts a free license to kill. You're sick."

Benedict wanted to keep the other man talking, at least for a few minutes more until he could bandage his leg. The shirt was sticky with blood and he couldn't knot it in place with his left hand. "You must be sick to come here," he said. "What other reason could you possibly have?" He laid the gun down silently, then fumbled with haste to bandage the wound.

"Sickness is relative," the voice in the darkness said, "as is crime. Man invents societies and the rules of his invented societies determine the crimes. *O tempora! O mores!* Homosexuals in Periclean Greece were honored men, and respected for their love. Homosexuals in industrial England were shunned and prosecuted for a criminal act. Who commits the crime—society or the man? Which of them is the criminal? You may attempt to argue a higher authority than man, but that would be only an abstract predication and what we are discussing here are realities. The law states that you are a criminal. I am here to enforce that law." The thunder of his gun added punctuation to his words and long splinters of wood flew from the doorframe. Benedict jerked the knot tight and grabbed up his pistol again.

"I do invoke a higher authority," he said. "Natural law,

the sanctity of life, the inviolability of marriage. Under this authority I wed and I love, and my children are the blessings of this union."

"Your blessings—and the blessings of the rest of mankind—are consuming this world like locusts," Mortimer said. "But that is an observation. First I must deal with your arguments.

"*Primus.* The only natural law is written in the sedimentary rocks and the spectra of suns. What you call natural law is man-made law and varies with the varieties of religion. Argument invalid.

"*Secundus.* Life is prolific and today's generations must die so that tomorrow's may live. All religions have the faces of Janus. They frown at killing and at the same time smile at war and capital punishment. Argument invalid.

"*Ultimus.* The forms of male and female union are as varied as the societies that harbor them. Argument invalid. Your higher authority does not apply to the world of facts and law. Believe in it if you wish, if it gives you satisfaction, but do not invoke it to condone your criminal acts."

"Criminal!" Benedict shouted, and fired two shots through the doorway, then cringed as an answering storm of bullets crackled by. Dimly, through the bathroom door, he heard the baby crying, awakened by the noise. He dropped out the empty shells and angrily pulled live cartridges from his pocket and jammed them into the cylinder. "You're the criminal, who is trying to murder me," he said. "You are the tool of the criminals who invade my house with their unholy laws and tell me I can have no more children. You cannot give me orders about this."

"What a fool you are," Mortimer sighed. "You are a social animal and do not hesitate to accept the benefits of your society. You accept medicine, so your children live now as they would have died in the past, and you accept a ration of food to feed them, food you do not even work for. This suits you, so you accept. But you do not accept planning for your family and you attempt to reject it. It is impossible. You must accept all or reject all. You must leave your society—or abide by its rules. You eat the food, you must pay the price."

"I don't ask for more food. The baby has its mother's

milk; we will share our food ration . . ."

"Don't be fatuous. You and your irresponsible kind have filled this world to bursting with your get, and still you will not stop. You have been reasoned with, railed against, cajoled, bribed and threatened, all to no avail. Now you must be stopped. You have refused all aid to prevent your bringing one more mouth into this hungry world, and, since you have done so anyway, you are to be held responsible for closing another mouth and removing it from this same world. The law is a humane one, rising out of our history of individualism and the frontier spirit, and gives you a chance to defend your ideals with a gun. And your life."

"The law is not humane," Benedict said. "How can you possibly suggest that? It is harsh, cruel, and pointless."

"Quite the contrary, the system makes very good sense. Try to step outside yourself for a moment, forget your prejudices and look at the problem that faces our race. The universe is cruel—but it's not ruthless. The conservation of mass is one of the universe's most ruthlessly enforced laws. We have been insane to ignore it so long, and it is sanity that now forces us to limit the sheer mass of human flesh on this globe. Appeals to reason have never succeeded in slowing the population growth, so, with great reluctance, laws have been passed. Love, marriage, and the family are not affected—up to a reasonable maximum of children. After that a man *voluntarily* forsakes the protection of society, and must take the consequences of his own acts. If he is insanely selfish, his death will benefit society by ridding it of his presence. If he is not insane and has determination and enough guts to win—well then, he is the sort of man that society needs and he represents a noble contribution to the gene pool. Good and law-abiding citizens are not menaced by these laws."

"How dare you!" Benedict shouted. "Is a poor, helpless mother of an illegitimate baby a criminal?"

"No, only if she refuses all aid. She is even allowed a single child without endangering herself. If she persists in her folly, she must pay for her acts. There are countless frustrated women willing to volunteer for battle to even the score. They, like myself, are on the side of the law and eager to enforce it. So close my mouth, if you can,

Benedict, because I look forward with pleasure to closing your incredibly selfish one."

"Madman!" Benedict hissed and felt his teeth grate together with the intensity of his passion. "Scum of society. This obscene law brings forth the insane dregs of humanity and arms them and gives them license to kill."

"It does that, and a useful device it is, too. The maladjusted expose themselves and can be watched. Better the insane killer coming publicly and boldly than trapping and butchering your child in the park. Now he risks his life and whoever is killed serves humanity with his death."

"You admit you are a madman—a licensed killer?" Benedict started to stand but the hall began to spin dizzily and grow dark: he dropped back heavily.

"Not I," Mortimer said tonelessly. "I am a man who wishes to aid the law and wipe out your vile, proliferating kind."

"You're an invert then, hating the love of man and woman."

The only answer was a cold laugh that infuriated Benedict.

"Sick!" he screamed. "Or mad. Or sterile, incapable of fathering children of your own and hating those who can . . ."

"That's enough! I've talked enough to you, Benedict. Now I shall kill you."

Benedict could hear anger for the first time in the other's voice and knew that he had goaded the man with the prod of truth. He was silent, sick and weak, the blood still seeping through his rough bandage and widening in a pool on the floor. He had to save what little strength he had to aim and fire when the killer came through the doorway. Behind him he heard the almost silent opening of the bathroom door and the rustle of footsteps. He looked up helplessly into Maria's tear-stained face.

"Who's there with you?" Mortimer shouted, from where he crouched behind the armchair. "I hear you whispering. If your wife is there with you, Benedict, send her away. I won't be responsible for the cow's safety. You've brought this upon yourself, Benedict, and the time has now come to pay the price of your errors, and I shall be the instrumentality of that payment."

He stood and emptied the remainder of the magazine of bullets through the doorway, then pressed the button to release the magazine and hurled it after the bullets, clicking a new one instantly into place. With a quick pull he worked the slide to shove a live cartridge into the chamber and crouched, ready to attack.

This was it. He wouldn't need the knife. Walk a few feet forward. Fire through the doorway, then throw in the tear-gas pen. It would either blind the man or spoil his aim. Then walk through firing with the trigger jammed down and the bullets spraying like water and the man would be dead. Mortimer took a deep, shuddering breath—then stopped and gaped as Benedict's hand snaked through the doorway and felt its way up the wall.

It was so unexpected that for a moment he didn't fire, and when he did fire he missed. A hand is a difficult target for an automatic weapon. The hand jerked down over the light switch and vanished as the ceiling lights came on.

Mortimer cursed and fired after the hand and fired into the wall and through the doorway, hitting nothing except insensate plaster and feeling terribly exposed beneath the glare of light.

The first shot from the pistol went unheard in the roar of his gun and he did not realize that he was under fire until the second bullet ripped into the floor close to his feet. He stopped shooting, spun around, and gaped.

On the fire escape outside the broken window stood the woman. Slight and wide-eyed and swaying as though a strong wind tore at her, she pointed the gun at him with both hands and jerked the trigger spasmodically. The bullets came close but did not hit him, and in panic he pulled the machine pistol up, spraying bullets in an arc toward the window. "Don't! I don't want to hurt you!" he shouted even as he did it.

The last of his bullets hit the wall and his gun clicked and locked out of battery as the magazine emptied. He hurled the barren metal magazine away and tried to jam a full one in and the pistol banged again and the bullet hit him in the side and spun him about. When he fell the gun fell from his hand. Benedict, who had been crawling slowly and painfully across the floor, reached him at the same moment and clutched at his throat with hungry fingers.

"Don't . . ." Mortimer croaked and thrashed about. He had never learned to fight and did not know what else to do.

"Please, Benedict, don't," Maria said, climbing through the window and running to them. "You're killing him."

"No—I'm not," Benedict gasped. "No strength. My hands are too weak."

Looking up he saw the pistol near his head and he reached and tore it from her.

"One less mouth now!" he shouted and pressed the hot muzzle against Mortimer's chest and pulled the trigger and the muffled shot tore into the man, who kicked violently once and died.

"Darling, you're all right?" Maria wailed, kneeling and clutching him to her.

"Yes . . . all right. Weak, but that's from losing the blood, I imagine, but the bleeding has stopped now. It's all over. We've won. We'll have the food ration now, and they won't bother us anymore and everyone will be satisfied."

"I'm so glad," she said, and actually managed to smile through her tears. "I really didn't want to tell you before, not bother you with all this other trouble going on. But there's going to be . . ." She dropped her eyes.

"What?" he asked incredulously. "You can't possibly mean . . ."

"But I do." She patted the rounded mound of her midriff. "Aren't we lucky?"

All he could do was look up at her, his mouth wide and gaping like some helpless fish cast up on the shore.

FAMOUS FIRST WORDS

Millions of words of hatred, vitriol, and polemic have been written denigrating, berating, and castigating the late Professor Ephraim Hakachinik, and I feel that the time has come when the record must be put straight. I realize that I too am risking the wrath of the so-called authorities by speaking out like this, but I have been silent too long. I must explain the truth as my mentor explained it to me, because only the truth, lunatic as it may sound, can correct the false impressions that have become the accepted coin in reference to the professor.

Let me be frank: early in our relationship I, too, felt that the professor was—how shall we call it—eccentric even beyond the accepted norm for the faculty of backwater universities. In appearance he was a most untidy man, almost hidden behind a vast mattress of tangled beard that he affected for the dual purpose of saving the trouble and the expense of shaving and of dispensing with the necessity of wearing a necktie. This duality of purpose was common in almost everything he did; I am sure that simultaneous professorships in both the arts and the sciences is so rare as to be almost unique, yet he occupied two chairs at Miskatonic University, those of quantum physics and conversational Indo-European. This juxtaposition of abilities undoubtedly led to the perfection of his invention and to the discovery of the techniques needed to develop its possibilities.

As a graduate student I was very close to Professor Hakachinik and was present at the very moment when the germ of an idea was planted that was to flower eventually into the tremendous growth of invention that was to be his contribution to the sum of knowledge of mankind. It was a sunny June afternoon, and I am forced to admit that I was dozing over a repetitious (begat, begat, begat) fragment of the Dead Sea Scrolls when a hoarse shout echoed from the paneled walls of the library and shocked me awake.

"Neobičan!" the professor exclaimed again—he has a tendency to break into Serbo-Croatian when excited—and a third time, "Neobičan!"

"What is wonderful, Professor?" I asked.

"Listen to this quotation—it is inspirational—from Edward Gibbon; he was visiting Rome, and this is what he wrote: *'As I sat musing amidst the ruins of the Capitol, while the barefooted friars were singing vespers in the Temple of Jupiter . . . the idea of writing the decline and fall of the city first started to my mind.'*

"Isn't that wonderful, my boy, simply breathtaking, a real historical beginning if I ever heard one. It all started there and, twelve years and five hundred thousand words later, wracked by writer's cramp, Gibbon scribbled *The End* and dropped his pen. *The History of the Decline and Fall of the Roman Empire* was finished. Inspiring!"

"Inspiring?" I asked dimly, my head still rattling with *begats*.

"Dolt!" he snarled, and added a few imprecations in Babylonian that will not bear translation in a modern journal. "Have you no sense of perspective? Do you not see that every great event in this universe must have had some tiny beginning?"

"That's rather an obvious observation," I remarked.

"Imbécil!" he muttered through clenched teeth. "Do you not understand the grandeur of the concept! The mighty redwood, reaching for the sky, and so wide in the trunk that it is pierced with a tunnel for motor vehicles to be driven through; this goliath of the forests was once a struggling, single-leafed shrub incapable of exercising a tree's peculiar attractions for even the most minuscule of dogs. Do you find this concept a fascinating one?"

I mumbled something incoherent to cover up the fact that I did not, and as soon as Professor Hakachinik had turned away I resumed my nap and forgot the matter completely for a number of days, until I received a message summoning me to the professor's chambers.

"Look at that," he said, pointing to what appeared to be a normal radio, housed in a crackle-gray cabinet and faced with a splendid display of knobs and dials.

"Bully!" I said, with enthusiasm. "We will listen to the final game of the World Series together."

"Stumpfsinnig Schwein!" he growled. "That is no ordinary radio, it is an invention of mine embodying a new concept, my Temporal Audio Psychogenetic detector—TAP for short—and 'tap' is what it does. By utilizing a theory and technique that are so far beyond your rudimentary powers of comprehension that I will make no attempt to explain them, I have constructed my TAP to detect and amplify the voices of the past so that they can be recorded. Listen and be amazed!"

The professor switched on the device and, after a few minutes of fiddling with the dials, exacted from the loudspeaker what might be described as a human voice mouthing harsh animal sounds.

"What was that?" I asked.

"Protomandarin of the latter part of the thirteenth century B.C., obviously," he mumbled, hard at work again on the dials, "but just idle chatter about the rice crop, the barbarians from the south, and such. That is the difficulty; I have to listen to volumes of that sort of thing before I chance on an authentic beginning and record it. But I have been doing just that—and succeeding!" He slapped his hand on a loose pile of scrawled pages that stood upon the desk. "Here are my first successes, fragmentary as yet, but I'm on the way. I have traced a number of important events back to their sources and recorded the very words of their originators at the precise moment of inception. Of course the translations are rough—and quite colloquial—but that can be corrected later. My study of beginnings has begun."

I'm afraid I left the professor's company then—I did want to hear the ball game—and regret to say that it was the last time that I—or anyone—ever saw him alive. The sheets of paper he so valued were taken to be the ravings of an unwell mind, their true worth misunderstood, and they were discarded. I have salvaged some of them and now present them to the public, who can truly judge their real worth. Fragmentary as they are, they cast the strong light of knowledge into many a darkened corner of history that has been obscured in the past.

". . . even though it is a palace it is still my home, and it is too small by far with my new stepmother, who is a *bitz*.* I had hoped to continue in my philosophy studies, but it is impossible here. Guess I better run the army down to the border; there may be trouble there . . ."

Alexander of Macedonia—336 B.C.

". . . hot is not Ye word for it, and alle of VIRGINIA is like an Oven this summer. When Opportunity arose to earn a little l.s.d. running a Survey line through the hills I grabbed it before M.F. could change his Minde. That is how I met . . . . today (forgot his name, must ask him tomorrow) in the Taverne. We did have an Ale together and did both complain mightily upon the Heat. With one thing leading to Another as they are wont to do, we had more Ales and he did Confide in me. He is a member of a secret club named, I *think* since Memory is hazy here, The Sons of Liberty, or some such . . ."

George Washington—1765

"France has lost its greatness when an honest inventor gains no profit from his onerous toil. I have neglected my practice for months now, perfecting my Handy Hacker Supreme Salami Slicer. I should have earned a fortune selling the small models to every butcher in France. But no!—the Convention uses the large model without paying a sou to me, and the butchers are naturally reluctant now to purchase . . ."

J. I. Guillotin, M.D.—1791

"My head doth ache as though I suffereth an ague, and if I ever chance on the slippery-fingered soddish son of an ill-tempered whore who dropped that night-vessel in Fetter Lane, I will roundly thrash him to within an inch of his life, and perhaps a bit beyond. Since arrival in London I have learned the neatness of step and dexterity of motion

---

* Thought to refer to the *peetz*, a small desert bird, but the reference is obscure.

needed to avoid the contents of the many vessels emptied into the street, but this is the first time there was need to dodge the container itself. Had I moved a trifle quicker this body of crockery in motion would have continued in motion. But my head doth ache. As soon as it is better I must think on this; there is the shade of an idea here."

Sir Isaac Newton—1682

"I. is afraid that F. knows! If he does I have had it. If I. was not so seductively attractive I would find someone else's bed, but she does lead me on so. She says she can sell some of her jewelry and buy those three ships she was looking at. The last place I want to go is to the damn Spice Islands, right now at the height of the Madrid season. But F. *is* king, and if he finds out . . . !"

(Attributed to Cristoforo Colombo
of Genoa, 1492, but derivation
is obscure.)

"Am I glad I got little Pierre the Erector Set. As soon as he is asleep I'll grab the funny tower he just made. I know the Exposition Committee won't use anything like this, but it will keep them quiet for a while."

Alexandre Gustave Eiffel—1888

"Woe unto China! Crop failures continue this year and the depression is getting worse. Millions unemployed. The only plan that seems at all workable is this construction project that Wah Ping-ah is so hot about. He says it will give a shot in the arm to the economy and get the cash circulating again. But what a screwball idea! Build a wall fifteen hundred miles long! He wants to use his own initials and call it the WPA project, but I'm going to call it something different and tell the people it's to keep the barbarians out, as you can always sell them on defense appropriations if you scare them enough."

Emperor Shih Hwang-ti—252 B.C.

"There will be a full moon tonight so I'll have enough light to find that balcony. I hate to take a chance going near that crazy family, but Maria is the hottest piece of baggage in town! She made her kid sister Julie—the buck-

toothed wonder!—promise to have the window unlocked."
Romeus Montague—1562

(Extract from the ship's log.) "Made a landfall today on a hunk of rock. What navigation! We head for Virginia and end up in Massachusetts! If I ever catch the Quaker brat who stole the compass . . . ! ! !"
The brig *Mayflower*—1620

There are many more like this, but these samples will suffice to prove that Professor Hakachinik was a genius far ahead of his time, and a man to whom the students of history owe an immeasurable debt.

Since there have been many rumors about the professor's death, I wish to go on record now and state the entire truth. I was the one who discovered the professor's body, so I know whereof I speak. It is a lie and a canard that the good man committed suicide; indeed he was in love with life and was cut off in his prime, and I'm sure he looked forward to many more productive years. Nor was he electrocuted, though his TAP machine was close by and fused and melted as though a singularly large electrical current had flowed through it. The official records read heart failure and for want of a better word this description will have to stand, though in all truth the cause of death was never determined. The professor appeared to be in fine health and in the pink of condition, though of course he was dead. Since his heart was no longer beating, heart failure seemed to be a satisfactory cause of death to enter in the records.

In closing let me state that when I discovered the professor he was seated at his desk, his head cocked toward the loudspeaker and his pen clutched in his fingers. Under his hand was a writing pad with an incomplete entry—what he appeared to be writing when death struck. I make no conclusions about this, but merely record it as a statement of fact.

The writing is in Old Norse, which, for the benefit of those not acquainted with this interesting language, I have translated into modern English:

". . . this meeting will come to order and if you don't put those mead horns away there'll be a few cracked skulls around here, I tell you. Now, order of business. There have been some reports of tent caterpillars in Yggdrasill and some dead branches, but we'll get onto that later. Of more pressing interest is the sandy concrete that has been found cracking in the foundations of Bifrost Bridge. I want to—just one moment—this is supposed to be a closed meeting and there is someone listening in. Thor, will you please take care of that eavesdropper . . ."

A SELECTION OF BESTSELLERS FROM *SPHERE*

FICTION

A PERFECT STRANGER	Danielle Steel	£1.75 ☐
MISSING PERSONS	C. Terry Cline Jr	£1.95 ☐
A GREEN DESIRE	Anton Myrer	£2.50 ☐
FLOODTIDE	Suzanne Goodwin	£1.95 ☐
JADE TIGER	Craig Thomas	£2.25 ☐

FILM & TV TIE-INS

THE YEAR OF LIVING DANGEROUSLY	C. J. Koch	£1.75 ☐
STAR WARS	George Lucas	£1.75 ☐
FAME	Leonore Fleischer	£1.75 ☐
UPSTAIRS, DOWNSTAIRS	John Hawkesworth	£1.50 ☐

NON-FICTION

A QUESTION OF BALANCE	H.R.H. The Duke of Edinburgh	£1.50 ☐
THE DEATH OF THE DIAMOND	Edward Jay Epstein	£1.95 ☐
SUSAN'S STORY	Susan Hampshire	£1.75 ☐
SECOND LIFE	Stephani Cook	£1.95 ☐
YOU CAN TEACH YOUR CHILD INTELLIGENCE	David Lewis	£1.95 ☐

All Sphere books are available at your local bookshop or newsagent, or can be ordered direct from the publisher. Just tick the titles you want and fill in the form below.

Name _____

Address _____

_____

Write to Sphere Books, Cash Sales Department, P.O. Box 11, Falmouth, Cornwall TR10 9EN

Please enclose cheque or postal order to the value of the cover price plus:

UK: 45p for the first book, 20p for the second and 14p per copy for each additional book ordered to a maximum charge of £1.63.

OVERSEAS: 75p for the first book and 21p for each additional book.

BFPO & EIRE: 45p for the first book, 20p for the second book plus 14p per copy for the next 7 books, thereafter 8p per book.

Sphere Books reserve the right to show new retail prices on covers which may differ from those previously advertised in the text or elsewhere, and to increase postal rates in accordance with the PO.